Other Books in The Vintage Library
of Contemporary World Literature

Blood of
Requited Love

Blood of Requited Love

Manuel Puig

TRANSLATED FROM
THE SPANISH
BY JAN L. GRAYSON

AVENTURA

The Library of Contemporary World Literature

VINTAGE BOOKS   A DIVISION OF RANDOM HOUSE   NEW YORK

An Aventura Original, July 1984.

English translation Copyright © 1984 by Jan L. Grayson

All rights reserved under International and Pan-American
Copyright Conventions. Published in the United States by
Random House, Inc., New York, and simultaneously in
Canada by Random House of Canada Limited, Toronto.
Originally published in Spain as Sangre de Amor
Correspondido by Editorial Seix Barral, S.A.,
Barcelona in 1982. Copyright © 1982 by Manuel Puig.

Library of Congress Cataloging in Publication Data

Puig, Manuel.

Blood of requited love.

Translation of: Sangre de amor correspondido.

I. Title.

PQ7798.26.u4s213 1984   863   83–40385

ISBN 0-394-72440-2

Manufactured in the United States of America

First American Edition

Blood of Requited Love

Chapter One

—When was the last time you saw me?

He saw her for the last time ten, eight years ago. After that, only from afar. It was in Cocotá, the State of Rio. In the park, next to the church, right? She went to meet him, they had a date, or—how was it? From there they left together, to the Municipal Club to dance all night. And what else happened with her? They were at the dance until two-thirty in the morning, then they went to a hotel to do their business, is that clear? That night.

—And no one noticed that a girl of fifteen was going to a hotel?

There were a lot of people in the club, the town wasn't very big, six thousand people, six thousand inhabitants. But it was possible to go to a hotel, no problem—not

there, but in another town nearby, is that clear? They
arrived, had a little beer, and so on. They went by car,
back then he had a Maverick. Later, after he hit the skids,
he never had a car again. Next year, God willing, he's
going to buy one on credit.

—What dance was that?

It was a dance with all Roberto Carlos music, nothing
else, all night long Roberto Carlos records. There were
also other places to make out. There was the swimming
pool, for some terrific dips, and the waterfall. They
climbed on the rocks, a waterfall full of rocks, they put
on bikini and bathing shorts and went into the trees—
right there is the real jungle.

—I asked you about the dance, about the dance that
night.

The dance was jam-packed, three or four thousand
people. The two of them knew a lot of people, so many,
but it was getting late, time to get moving. She had waited
for him in the park, she usually waited for him there—
there or at the exit of the church, because she was very
Catholic. If everything was going well she'd wait for him
every night at the church door. At eight in the evening,
generally. And from there they'd make their way, even-
tually, to her house, or if not there, to an aunt's house.
And they'd stay there, and they'd serve him a little coffee
or a steak, one of those huge ones that he liked. That kind
of thing. He'd stay until about twelve at night. In her
house, her mother's house. She was there, with her mother
and her grandmother. And no one else. She had a father,
but he usually arrived around one in the morning. He

was a traveling salesman and he didn't arrive until then, but before that her brother would usually show up— Paulo, Paulo Rossi was his name, wasn't it? He'd come more or less about that time, about midnight, because during that period he was also a soccer player. But he wasn't the best. In the Cocotá Sports Club. Amateur soccer, they didn't get paid. Every Sunday at three-fifteen in the afternoon. And they trained every Wednesday and Thursday until five. Until the night of the dance, that Saturday night, when they went to the hotel. At the dance they were feeling terrific, satisfied, happy with life.

—And what did we talk about at that dance? I want to see if you're telling me the truth.

They talked about love, nothing but sweet talk. A little kissing, he made a few moves, and then some more, to get them to leave the dance, because until then they'd never had a chance to go to a hotel because she was still very young, a virgin, is that clear? And that Saturday it all started, she had a few drinks and they went to the hotel, and well, that was the last time he saw her, isn't that right? That night of the dance and the next day. It was on the way back, returning from Floresta de Cocotá to Cocotá itself, which is another town, it was then that he made a date with her for eight-thirty the following evening, which was Sunday, at her house. But he didn't arrive until a quarter past eleven that night, and they stayed up talking, and fighting, and arguing. He wanted to escape from her, and the whole world was coming down on him—the mother, the grandmother were on his back, "Don't abandon my daughter!" That whole story, and he always slipping away, "No! I want to travel, I have to make my own way in life! After that, I'll come back for sure. . . ." But he never came back. In all this time he never came around these parts, except once, in passing, isn't that so?

—That time you returned, could you see me from so far away?

That time he returned it seemed to him that he saw her; she tried to get closer, but he moved away, right? But the next time he's passing through, he'll try to say something nice to her, drop a friendly word, just casually, is that clear? Just to ease that mental problem of hers, she hadn't been well in the head, everyone said. That was what her mother had asked, "I know there's nothing more between you now, but you have to talk with her a little, what would it cost you?" The mother asked him to exchange a few words with her daughter, as a friend, call to her from that pretty gate of hers to chat, come down to her house, talk about whatever. And reminisce and then well, ask her, some way or another, to forgive him for staying away so long, etcetera, etcetera. Because she never married, he knows that, she's still not married—who would marry a woman who's screwed up in the head? He's sure that she's had hardly any boyfriends even, because no one ever saw her with anyone. He remembers everything about that last night at the dance, down to the last detail. She showed up in a new green dress, but he wasn't to be outdone. He showed up in a pair of Lee jeans that had just come out then, and a Round the World shirt. It was a very good-looking shirt, very few people had them then,

because they were expensive, is that clear? Why that
name? Who knows, at that time, they were selling them
all over the world, that's probably why they called them
Round the World. They arrived at the dance and began
to chat, everything was on track, up to that moment they
were getting along better than ever, he kept insisting that
they leave the dance to be alone, "My sweet, I want your
love, I want to get married, understand? But it can't be
right away." Because at that time he had nothing, is that
clear? He was penniless, but he knew what life was about
and he wanted to get out of that town, right? Then she insisted that he play soccer in the town. She wanted him to
study and play soccer in town.

—What was it I wanted you to be? Don't lie to
me.

At that time she wanted him to be . . . an engineer, at
that time, but he didn't have the means, is that clear
enough? His parents didn't have any money at that time.
Then he told her that he couldn't, that he had to blaze his
own trail in life; at that time what he did was . . . electrical projects, wasn't it? He studied, he studied a lot, about
electrical projects, then she'd usually insist that he study
even more, and it always came back to the same thing.
Then he would say, "It's not possible financially," and
she would say that she would help him, and it came back
to the same thing, is that clear? He'd tell her, "Baby, it
can't happen, it's really impossible for me, I don't have
the capital." And they never got over this problem, one
minute they'd talk about soccer, the next they were back
to the topic of studying and how much it cost, and she

said she'd ask her own father to pay for his studies. He said no, he wouldn't accept, for him it wasn't important up to that point. He wanted to shape his own life, is that clear? At a certain hour they left the dance. Because that night she felt that he was really serious about leaving town, that was when she gave it to him, thinking that that way she'd bind him to her, "You're not leaving at all, you're staying here with me, aren't you?" Then he told her no, he was still leaving, is it clear how it went? But the truth is he didn't tell her he was going to abandon her that night, he knew her weak spots very well, he'd die before he'd tell her a thing like that. The important thing was to get her out of the dance, outside he'd take care of the rest. The next day, sure he'd tell her. After this night had passed. It never occurred to him that she'd go wrong in the head. Then he put her in the car, already talking about the subject, "My love, we're going to another town, to enjoy something new, what the hell. At last count we've been going together for three years, that's why I think I deserve a little trust," etcetera. She said that she wasn't going to give him anything. So he said that then everything was over, that he didn't understand what her intentions were. Then she cried, she broke into loud sobs, but he didn't give an inch, he was going full steam, he'd had a few too many, right? They stayed on that road. He humped her like crazy.

—In the hotel?

One night, no more, in that hotel. She asks him, she pleads that they can go back to being sweethearts whenever he comes back to town. She wants to go out with him, no matter what, she looks for him, she sends him messages, little notes, and he always dodges her. He goes out to meet some friends, is that clear? In that town so full of trees and little parks. And suddenly this little note finds him, "Hi! How are you? I always remember that night. I'm waiting for you on that bench, the one right in this same park," signed María da Gloria. Yes, sure he remembers, but it's not possible, he doesn't even return the note or anything, is that understood?

—They say one time you took me alone into the woods, far out in the country, is that true?

It was the brunette that he took to the woods, a very different question. The blond he took to the hotel, María da Gloria. Here's what happened: they got into the room, they took a shower, right? There was no way she'd take off her clothes. He started getting angry. He grabbed her hard, "No!" she screamed, "Get in bed, I tell you!" He threw her on the bed and took off her clothes, and they began to kiss and bite each other, and that kind of thing. She was crying like crazy, desperately. It was then that he chose to speak, "Baby, it's useless, you're not going to escape from here, the night is yours so grab it." And so on, there was no stopping his babbling. They had been going together for three years, what the hell, she owed it to him, and he wasn't going to let her give it to somebody else. Let's say he left her as he had planned to, and another guy came around and made her, then the joke would be on him, after three years of going together, is that clear? That's why he talked this way to her. And he taught her how things were done, he put her underneath, he put her on top, he bit her all over, he made her suck all of him, lick him everywhere, is that clear? It was a complete orgy, right? They did everything, all kinds of stuff, at one point she'd cry, then she'd laugh, she even tossed a few drinks down.

—That's not true, I've never drunk in my life. Liquor upsets me, I vomit right away, or I get a very bad headache.

It was Barbante whiskey, Dubar cognac, the best drinks to make her lose her head, is that clear? One after another she drank. Beer and some soft drinks before in the club, a lot of beer, one gets very thirsty with so many people in there and the dancing. Then they left. And at two-fifteen in the morning, he dropped her off at her house. But as he was leaving he saw another woman waiting on the pavement across the street. A neighbor of hers who had been waiting for him, without his knowing. As he passed the woman she called him, "Psst! . . . Hi, how are you?" And he stayed with her. He finished the little that was left of the night sleeping in this other woman's house.

—After you were with me in the hotel? That's not true.

He still had a lot of energy, he was like a stallion then, eighteen, or a little older, going full blast, right? It was just great, no kidding. Eight or ten beers at the dance, then the Dubar cognac, one of the most expensive drinks at that time. Very popular in Brazil, extremely popular, now it seems like it doesn't exist anymore, at least you don't hear about it. Or it only exists in those shit towns, is that clear? But he, with all that beer inside him, he wasn't debilitated, it was beyond belief, he banged her with all he had, he could go on for four hours with his gun cocked. No doubt about it. Sure there had been other important nights before for the two of them, carnival nights. Because they always went to these celebrations together.

—But why didn't anyone at home realize it, what had happened that night?

Few would remember that night now, it was Saturday, or better say Sunday. What else happened? When they arrived at her house they invited him to lunch the next day, there at the house, at one in the afternoon, before the soccer game. It was the day he was going to break up with her and play his last game for the town team, the Cocotá Sports Club.

—The last game?

Because he was going to leave, he was never again going to be a part of the team or anything else. He planned it all by himself, the only one who knew about it was his mother. There she was with her hair all white, uncombed, a mess, it's that she can't lift her arms because of rheumatism. He told her he was leaving and his mother stood there looking at him seriously, but then she let out a laugh. Then he said, "You look like a battered hen with that white hair all frizzy and messy, what do I have so many sisters for if they can't even fix you up a little?" His mother is good, if no one gets in her way, its the battered hens that peck you so that you bleed. He was already at María da Gloria's house for lunch at a quarter to one, right? A special lunch, is that clear? A lot of delicious things, chicken, shrimp, noodles—a big spread

—a salad with lettuce, tomatoes, the works. Here's what happened: they were all seated, he, her father, her mother and her hanging around his neck, and then she looked at her mother and said, "I'm very sorry, mama, but I love this boy, I love him with all my heart and nothing is going to separate us." And then her mother said, "I know that already, this young man drives you crazy." They continued talking, he always making them respect him, as usual, even though he was the poorest. And then he said, "Baby, the situation is as follows: I love you too, really, I love you a lot, I love you profoundly." He really did like her, is that clear?

—You didn't come to eat chicken and shrimp that Sunday. No one invited you.

God knows if she remembers all these things, with that sickness that came over her. She always wrote him letters, to the town of Baurú where he had gone, but he never answered, he was working for the electric company. For ECSP, Electric Company of the State of São Paulo. She always wrote to him, right? And then another problem arose, after lunch, that fantastic lunch, when it turned three and he was leaving for the soccer field, the game began at three-fifteen. It was the final game for the championship, the Sports Club of Cocotá against the Teixeira Nautical. She said to him then that he shouldn't go, not that day. And he answered, "Baby, the situation is as follows: Today I am going to play well, brilliantly." And she answered, "If that's the way it is, then I'm not going; I don't want to see you play brilliantly, like you've always played." He told her she could do whatever she pleased, and he left. In that game he made five goals. The only five goals of the game were the ones he made. He was riding high that afternoon. The females were besides themselves, lots of them, many who liked him then, friends of hers, classmates, who liked to talk to him and flirt on the sly, is that clear? And his two best friends, Donato, the halfback and Farelinho number ten, center-forward, were there also. All of the guys were his friends, but those two were especially good friends. And there was one other one who died later on, years ago now, that's why he'd forgotten about him, it had been a while since he'd thought of him. Then they went to celebrate after the game, they drank beer, a grand victory, a tremendous party, lots of females applauding in a bar that doesn't exist anymore. And afterward they went to her house to celebrate.

—That's not true, they wouldn't let you people into my house, I'm sure of that.

He told her he was already getting into the car and going to his farm, his mother's farm. And he left, he took a bath, and his mother had a premonition that he was going to leave, "Old girl, you already figured it out, I'm leaving tomorrow at six-thirty in the morning, so don't get scared on me, I can't go on living like this, I walk around without any money, and I need it for clothes, to have some elegance, some class; there are a lot of women out there looking for me and I need four or five shirts, four or five pairs of pants, and a bottle of perfume. Old girl, the situation is as follows: I'm only asking you for five cruzeiros. Back in those days that was really something, a five-cruzeiro bill. His mother told him that he couldn't leave with only that, what would he do later? He gave her a hug and he left and stayed out there until this day, now that he's pushing thirty-two, and that's all, sixteen hours by bus to Baurú, where ECSP placed a help-wanted ad. He hadn't even stepped off the bus yet when he wanted to return, he hadn't stopped thinking for a moment, already he began to miss the fans at the club's soccer games. He wanted to go back to Cocotá on the same bus, but he couldn't, he didn't have enough to pay for the return trip. And he hadn't slept the whole way, he'd been watching all the fields they crossed, which he'd never seen before. And what the fuck, the main thing is that he'd had fun, he'd put it good to her. Back in those days he didn't have so many problems, not even 10 percent of those he has today. Those that hadn't surfaced then have surfaced now. But she liked it a lot the first time. "You didn't like it that much because it hurt so bad, isn't that right?" "No, the situation is as follows: I should have paid attention to you, Josemar, and let you do this to me the first day I met you." And then and there he told her, "That's impossible because when I met you you were twelve years old, or younger? Back then you must have been ten years old. I would never have done that to you, is that clear? now, yes, you're at a good age, even though it hurt you just the same." He was crazy about her!

—I don't remember the pain, no matter how hard I try I can't remember.

It's hard to remember everything, she was fifteen going

on sixteen, he tries as hard as possible to forget her, if he talks a lot about that subject he gets the feeling that he wants to go see her, is that clear? He tries to forget. They spent many nights together making out, what the fuck, so many nights, they'd go stare at the moon and the stars. And things like that. First, they walked around the square, then by all the houses in the town, usually until midnight, they'd walk around, really, it's true that they walked around and during the daytime they'd go fishing. She was very scared of snakes, he used to grab those water cobras and throw them all over her, just to play around, alligators, recently born baby alligators. She was always afraid.

—If I was afraid, why did I allow myself to be locked in a hotel room?

At first no, but as soon as they began, yes, she was afraid. There she was, crying, because the pain was strong, is that clear? she was telling him no, no, no, until the final moment, and he was insisting, yes, yes. Because, as he told her, "If this business isn't taken care of to-night . . . it will never be taken care of. If you've been keeping this for me as you've always told me, then I want it today. If you don't give it to me today, I'll never want it again and I'll be annoyed forever." And the following night, Sunday night, he was with her from nine-fifteen, more or less, until after three in the morning, talking about nothing but that, you know, because in general she talked more than he did, no? because the woman usually talks more than the guy in such situations, "Josemar, I really love you, is that clear? all that I want is to be by your side, for me no other man exists, I used to love you, now I love you much more, isn't that right?" And he told her that it was useless to speak, he had really fallen for her, but without a cent he had to get away from there, or not? He never again gave her the pleasure of listening to her complaints. But that night he wounded her, he hurt her.

—You wounded me and hurt me?

She was crying, crying desperately, it was the first night, she had never suffered so, she had never been operated on for anything, and, really, it's something that wounds and hurts. He saw blood coming out, is that clear? a heavy flow of blood. He searched around and found her little panties on the bed, and with them he wiped the blood, with the panties themselves. The same little panties with the same label that all the women in town wore. And he drying the blood up nicely, cleaning her up. He'd wipe a little, then go into her again as far as he could. He didn't stop pushing until the whole thing was in. He didn't stop until he'd gotten everything in but his balls. He stopped there, of course. She was trembling, she was feeling cold, she'd tell him that she was feeling cold. He'd say to her, "So you've had enough, want me to take it out then?" And she'd say no, that he should persist, that he should keep going in, deeper each time. And there were no more problems, everything was in order. On the last night when they said good-bye, they went back to doing it, standing under a tree. He was saying good-bye to her, telling her that he was leaving. He wasn't coming back, he wasn't going to be with her, etcetera, and at the same time he'd tell her, "Baby, I'll be back, don't worry, the two of us will get married." And there they encrusted themselves again, standing, one more time, right? It was something out of the ordinary, very impressive. He seems to have forgotten what happened after that, he tried to forget and he doesn't remember anything anymore.

—Don't believe what they're saying about me.

It seems that ever since that night things started going to waste, because three years later he returned, and her mother spun around in the street and said to him, "Hello, Josemar." Her mother sent for him to call specifically so that he'd go talk to her. The grandmother, who was so good, very friendly toward him, already very old, was sick back then. The grandmother and the mother sent for him to tell him things like, "If you don't want to see her, if you don't want to talk to her, it's our business to see to it that she won't be there, she doesn't know that you've come back." He said, "Of course I'll come to your house, ma'am, but beg her not to show up, that way we'll be able to talk." And he was caught up in that situation for more than three hours, conversing with her mother, no?

—They never liked you in my house, the one who liked you was me.

Her mother kept on telling him, "The situation is as follows: I understand what you're saying, but don't abandon her, you have to come back to her, to see if she recovers and becomes right in the head, is that clear?

From the moment of the separation she lost her peace of mind, she became rebellious, nervous, hostile at home, she was rude to anyone who asked her anything; and later it got worse, the breakdown, madness, do you understand? and often she'd see you in her dreams; she'd say, 'I need Josemar! I need him! I adore him, I love him so. . . . I'll end up killing myself on account of him,' do you understand?" And he was in a difficult situation, considering that problem, right? and on the other hand, his own problem. And her mother would continue, "The worst is that she sees you almost every night when she goes to sleep, even though you're far away, in the state of São Paulo; and sometimes she sees you when she's awake; and always when she sees you she hears you telling her good things, sweet loving words, and that's why she can't forget you; if her nerves were all right, things would work themselves out, because all the girls of her age who fall in love . . . if the boy doesn't want them and goes to another town, little by little they get used to never seeing him again." Between the two problems, hers and his, what the fuck! he was better off taking care of his own, right? But in those days, he had a little bitch who was precious and who loved him, right? He was stuck not knowing what to do, it was useless, he had to go, he was frank with her mother, is that clear? He opened the book of his life to her, but without telling the worst because then there'd be a mess, not an awful mess, but more bullshit than anyone would imagine, because no one knew anything, it remained between him and her and that's that, everything in order. As he was leaving he turned around in the street and looked at her window, she wasn't there like before, waving good-bye until he turned down the street lined with those trees, those very tall ones.

—None of that is true. They never let you into my house, not then, not now.

Chapter Two

Where did he put those cigarettes? Sometimes when he changes his shirt he misplaces the pack and he has to have a nice cigarette right now. They wanted to get him away from her, they all did everything possible. They told her father he was a scoundrel, a loafer, and worse. She never believed what they said about him, right? and now that he doesn't see her he'd like her to know something, is that clear? That he's a decent person.

—Was I the same then as I am now? How did I wear my hair? I'm sure you won't remember.

She had long hair, blond, the daughter of Italians. But he can't find his matches, he has a lot of problems, the sick mother, they asked him for an estimate for putting all new tiles in an old apartment's bathroom and he gave

it and now the cost of the materials has gone up and he's
not going to make anything, he's in debt, hell, what kind
of a life is this, he likes to work as an electrician, not a
mason. And he can't find his matches, he has to smoke so
he can remember about all that stuff.

—People have to remember what really happened,
not the lies.

He remembers all that happened, is that clear? Only
what happened.

—Your mother is sick, who takes care of her when
you go to work?

He has to travel more than an hour from here to downtown Rio, he leaves early in the morning and gets back
late at night.

—Did you come here to live because the name is so
pretty? I like that name a lot, Santísimo.

He likes Santísimo a lot because it has clean air and a
lot of jungle that grows by itself, like in Cocotá.

—In my window there were none of those plants that
grow by themselves, only fancy plants that blossom.

Usually she'd just watch him from the window of her
room on the top floor, it was a pretty house, not humble
like other ones. Her father was a salesman, he sold all
kinds of shoes and clothes, he'd go out in the country to
sell all of his stuff. He brought stuff to town from São
Paulo and then he sold it door-to-door. He'd come by
bus with everything packed, in sacks. A house with a
big garden in front, and in back the vegetable garden.
And in front of the house were the two big guava trees,
but her window was on the side, and when he got there

he'd wait for her reclining against the trunk of the guava tree, the one on the left.

—Why did you always hide behind that tree?

He'd wait behind one of the trees, the one on the left, because they say that the left ball is the one that's most powerful, and the tree passes on the power, it passes it on to whoever is also male. When he'd leave she would watch him from the window until he disappeared, but while she watched he kept waving good-bye.

—So far it's all true, I'm sure of that.

The mother lived way out in the country, that last night he got there when it had already started to get light, a long way, like two hours by dirt road, he had to go on those roads with potholes, mud, the car would get stuck, he'd push, a hell of a confusion, there were cattle sleeping in the middle of the road, cows and calves, branches lying across the road, right? He'd sleep there, he'd get out, push the car until he could make out a person named Alcibíades, they called him Cibides, a farmhand of his father's. It's been years now since he saw him, "Something's happened I'm afraid, for you to arrive at this hour." He'd left María da Gloria at three in the morning, or three-thirty, and he was arriving close to six because the road was so long, almost three hours by foot, "Your face looks like you've heard bad news." And he answered, "Cibides my good friend, my good old friend." Because he always called him that, "My good friend, tomorrow, or in a little while, no one's going to see me around here anymore." But the other one didn't believe

him, Cibides was a friend of his father's, a very good
friend of the family, that's why he didn't believe anything he said. He left that morning without seeing anyone, he didn't even see his mother when leaving the
house, so as not to go spreading sadness.

—That's not true—wasn't it the case that she gave you
five cruzeiros and then you hugged her?

His mother wasn't home on Monday mornings.

—Your mother used to work in another house? She
left earlier than anyone to work as a servant in another
house?

She never worked outside her home, she always did
what's called domestic work, but in her own home. His
father was in the rice field already and he didn't see him
either, the father had cattle, calves, cows, hogs, hens,
guinea fowl, dogs. All the children had been born there
on the farm, and Josemar, who was the third, was too, in
spite of everything. His father used to work a lot, now
he's given it all up, the obligations fell on the shoulders
of the son and the mother, the father wasn't breaking his
back anymore, he'd changed, right? He hit the bottle.
Lost faith in life. Josemar was the handsomest child and
that always infuriated the father. Josemar left home. It
was the second time already he was being forced to leave.

—Now I have something to ask you, why have you
begun to think so much about me? For years you hardly
ever did, if you did at all.

There were eleven brothers and sisters, right? Although back then there weren't eleven yet, but there were

already a lot. There was the sister, the older brother, and he was the third, right? The thing is that at around four-thirty in the morning the father always woke him up to round up the cows and milk them, right? The cows were in the field in the rain, it was thundering loudly with lightning and everything, and the father would always point his finger at him to go out in that storm, he was no more than six years old. "You, Carminha, hell, let's go! it's time to send your child to round up the cows," and she'd say, "Which one of them?" And the smallest had to go, "Josemar, he's the one who has to bring them in." And he had to go, even though he was younger than the other two, it was always raining, he squeezed out the milk, after that he brought the calves to suckle, he brought the cows to where there was grass, and shrubs, while he was at it, to save himself the trouble of having to cut them himself, he weeded the grounds and tended the orange grove, everything, hunted birds, he was crazy about birds, he still is to this day. Canaries with colored chests, cardinals, blackbirds, he caught every kind of bird.

—What did you do to them once you had them in your hand?

If the bird was worth anything, if it could be tamed and could sing, he was very tender to it. If it was a stupid bird, ugly, he pulled its feathers out, he plucked it and let it go. Then one day his father caught him, by now he'd seen these plucked birds going naked many times, "Hell, don't do that to a poor animal, the little creatures must be left alone." And he said, "No you don't understand, I set the trap to catch this canary and another one came and pecked at it, it was a bad bird, a damned bird from hell." He set the plucked bird free and it flew away and that was that.

—Wouldn't that bird get sick in the head like me, or die?

They don't die because you pull out their feathers, they grow back. He even did it again, the bird came back and fell into the trap again, and he pulled out its feathers another time. He was like that. The worst thing is that his father had a machine for polishing rice, after the cows, then grazing and letting the horses loose in the field, weeding the grounds, which it always fell to him to do when he was little, he'd go to watch the rice machine and help out. No one was allowed to touch the machine, he was six years old, he'd sweep up and these guys would keep throwing the rice husks on the ground, he would hang around there, always around there, "Don't touch that machine! It's not something to play with!" Until around midnight the machine was set on fire. It burned up. The father thought he already knew who it was that set the machine on fire. "I was sleeping at that hour, I didn't go out to play with fire!" No one ever knew who'd done it. No one found out who it was, not even the insurance people, right?

—No, no one ever found out it was you.

The father got along well with the two oldest children, Fernanda and Zé, and after Josemar came another load of children. But he had a grudge against the third, treated him different from the rest, the kid didn't know why, sometimes the father also sent the other two to work, but the one he never spared was the third, most of all. That's why they fought so much—he, the father, and the children. They fought like crazy. It enraged the third child, because he could have sent the others to work, too, right? But the father thought the third kid had to do it all. No one knows why, to this day he still doesn't know why.

—He didn't love you because you were different from the others. And I know why you were different.

The third child was whiter, he didn't have the face of an Indian like the rest of them, he was even handsomer than the landowner's children, who were white like Josemar.

—I know very well why your father didn't like you.

It wasn't for anything special. Frankly, he never expected anything from the father. He expected everything from the mother, because the mother is as follows: the son can be the worst kind but she'll always stand by him, but in that case the son was very good, and one day he was waiting for one of the younger sisters to be born, Fátima, after him comes María Helena, then Aparecida and Nelson. And the adopted black, Zilmar, his friend and brother. So at that time the mother was confined, expecting, and he'd talked to an aunt about sending her a pile of clothes to wash and he said he wouldn't bring them because the wild cow was loose in the area and would come after him, "No, do what you're told, the cow doesn't attack anyone."

—I'm listening.

So he grabbed this pile of dirty clothes and the oldest brother, who was the most wily, opened his mouth, "We'll carry it between us, the two of us." And the father turned around and looked at the third child and told him he wanted those clothes washed and back by the day after tomorrow, without fail. So, hell, the oldest brother looked at him, "What you have to do is the following, Josemar, it's your turn to take the clothes to this place I'll tell you about, so when you get there I'll already be waiting there." He was a wily one, son of a bitch, he sent him to wait at the place where he'd seen the cow. So he went, hell, the third child took off. He had to go. OK, he went, with that big bundle, it was heavy, he lugged it, he dragged it however he could.

—He who is incapable of loving his father is incapable of loving anyone, right?

No sooner had he arrived then the cow went and attacked him, she gored him all over. To this day he has marks on his stomach, way down, and on his chest and in back on his shoulders.

—Where are the scars? I want you to show them to me, if they're higher than the belly button I want to see them.

He's suffered a lot in life! He fell rolling over with the cow, he grabbed onto it. Until he fell into a ditch, a ditch with poison ivy. He stayed there, covered all over with poison ivy, and she kept trampling him, stomping on him, biting him, and finally he stayed still, covering his head with his hands, what else could he do. From afar the father saw that the cow was attacking someone so he went running to see, it was attacking the kid. That's when the father scared it off.

—Your father was very good, do you realize that?

Then an idea occurred to the child, to him, alone, he recovered from those cow gores, no problem, in one month, more or less, they didn't even take him to the doctor, and within him that hatred began to grow, and the nerves, right? That's when it occurred to him to kill the cow. He said to himself, "I'm going to kill that cow." She didn't like people, no matter what she gave milk, a lot of milk, but she attacked people. The father was the one who milked her, she wouldn't do anything to the father.

—First I want you to tell me whether or not you hugged your mother before you left. I'm afraid you've forgotten the truth forever, as it happened to me once.

The father was the one the cow didn't do anything to. The third child would speak to himself at times, like crazy people, so while he was walking by himself he said, "It's OK, nothing's happened." So time passed, time passed for sure, more or less three or four months passed, he was cured, and what did he do? He climbed into the closet, grabbed the revolver and left for the showdown with the cow, and when she came at him to gore him he pointed it right at her head, between the two horns, he squeezed the trigger and bang! Two shots to the head, he killed the cow. Then all the fury of the head of the household was unleashed, right? The father gave him a beating for everything, present, past, and future, but the cow was done with. It really happened like that, and then the father began to pick on him even worse than before, just looking at the child would irritate him badly. Life came to be an endless war between the two of them when he began to see that his son was becoming stronger, a man already, one day he looked at him hard, "My son, the situation is as follows: you're becoming a man already, if you want to go your own way no one's stopping you." That is, the father was throwing him out, wasn't he? "OK, old man, I don't have anything to say about it, the one to decide is my mother." And she said, "No one is going to leave here, my son is as much mine as yours, and he's going to stay here like the rest of the children." The third child was the only one who defended the mother, and the mother defended him.

—It was all your mother's fault, isn't that true?

It seems that the old man sold the dead cow to the butcher, now that the cow was dead he opened her up and sold her to the butcher for his regular customers. He even brought some meat home to eat, and the third child wouldn't eat it because he hated her good, that animal had almost killed him, wasn't that so?

—The cow hated you because you were bad to her.

She didn't like kids, it was the same with all the smallest ones, the same thing. With the third she had a special problem because he had given her some tremendous beatings when he found her tied up. He disliked her from long before the goring. The old man tethered her so he could milk her and while he went to look for the bucket the third mounted her and shoved in his thing, he stuck it in to hurt her, shit whore! Zelinha was the cow's name, that bitch of a cow! Goddamn her, worse than dangerous, the way she gored! Left alone she'd knock down a strong wall, like one of these, with one of those butts! An evil whore, unbelievable, and clever like no one else. The fact is that the big problem between the father and mother was that the father had another woman. So it kept them in a constant state of warfare. A woman who lived there in the countryside, but not close by, younger than the other women the father had in town. He always had plenty of women, the father, is that clear? this one was single, and the third child tried to help, to put everything in its place. The mother didn't know what was going on but she suspected. The son was against the father and for the mother, he always said that to the mother, but not to the father, "Mama, don't pay any attention to that," and that type thing, "There's no reason to feel so bad." He was one of the few intelligent children, he wanted everything to be fine, no arguments, no battles, not the slightest fight in the household.

—But they used to say that . . .

But nothing. He doesn't have enough for another pack of cigarettes, and now he's got three left for the whole night. And he's going to light another one. He was about eleven years old when he discovered everything. He saw everything, got back home and told everything to his mother. He'd already imagined it but now he knew for sure. So he'd just confirmed it, he went up to the mother where no one else could hear, "The situation is as follows: he has another woman, that's why he never has any money left for you, do you realize? Is it clear now? Because he's giving money to the other woman, that kind of thing, do you understand what I'm saying? The business

is a real scandal." The third child was always loaded
down with problems, these things left him all fucked up.

—There are people who don't love anyone, your heart
is dried up inside.

Up to a certain time the father's heart wasn't dried up,
he'd been very good to the mother. Later he changed, the
person he'd been before, is that clear? "But now his
heart is dried up," the mother used to say, he'd changed
completely. But that was many years later, the third
child only doesn't want to tell more than the truth, he
always tried to defend her one way or another, is that
clear? And the day of the cow, the father had a fight with
the mother because he wanted to hit the third child and
the mother wouldn't let him. So then the father wanted to
hit her. She slipped away from him and went to a neighbor's house. Her name was Doña Olinda, and she said,
"Oh Lord, what's all this?" and that kind of thing, and
advice. "Ma'am, go back home." And who knows what
else she said, "I'll go with you, he won't do anything to
you." Then Doña Olinda took them to the house, right?
And they went inside, that whole business, no problem.
So this time when they arrived he had a nice welcome for
the whole world and everything, but it was really fake,
wasn't it? He was that kind of person, a fake, a traitor.
And no sooner had the other one left than he grabbed a
knife and wanted to kill the mother of the children.

—For having defended you, just for that? Around here
they say your mother was the wicked one, and that you
took after her.

So the mother jumped up, if she hadn't run she really

would have been in for it! All the kids were dying of fright, the whole brood, "I'll kill you, I'm going to kill you!" Luckily there was a mandarin tree not too far away, they ran to it and hid, there were a lot of trees to hide behind, but under the mandarin tree there are never any snakes, they don't like the smell of those oranges. Then he and the mother slept there that night. But the best tree on the farm was a different one, it was close to the house, too close. He liked that tree better than any other, it also gave off perfume, and it even gave water, it was at the edge of the canal and water bubbled up from under the roots, he'd lean on two branches, hold on tight, he wouldn't fall, the branches supported him while he lowered himself all the way down to drink the water. He told the mother that the mandarin tree didn't give water in case they got thirsty during the night, but the tree with the water was too close to the house. "And there might be a snake," the mother said. "Yes ma'am," he answered. They didn't go back to the house, they slept in the field. "Son, tomorrow we're going away from here, to Grandpa's house." Very far away, right? An unbelievable distance. More than three hours by foot and horseback to the mother's father's house, he's deceased by now. You could only go by foot or by horseback, "In the morning we'll go, we'll tell grandpa about these problems and we'll stay there until it's all straightened out." But before it got light she wanted to go into the house for a few clothes to cover themselves with, mother and child. Then the father saw her and threw himself on top of her and started to hit her, not with his fist but with his open hand, slapping her around hard, and when the child saw this he climbed onto the father's back and began pounding on him from behind and, without meaning to, he hit the mother too, a hell of a mess, until Cibides showed up and broke up the fight, he and the mother finally left, that much he remembers. Only she would remember the other details. They stayed there for eight days, with the grandfather, until the father showed up looking for them and talked them into coming back, everything was in order now, he said, they missed the mother at home, the rest of the brood did, it didn't matter to him, so that's when they left, "I'll always stand by you, ma'am, I promise." And to this day he always stands by her. In everything. No matter what. It's a family expense, like buying salt, because they had everything else on the farm, from rice to meat.

—Why do you call your mother ma'am? Didn't you love her either?

It was always sir and ma'am, ever since he was little he called everyone sir and ma'am. He still does. That's the way it was back then, not anymore, nowadays it's completely different, you call everyone in the world by their first name, and you swear at them. But the father had a grudge against the third child and an aunt was passing by and heard her sister Carminha complaining, "Astolfo has a terrible grudge against Josemarzinho, and I have to hit the child every now and then for no reason, it really makes me mad, he's eleven years old already and one of these days they're going to kill each other." And the aunt told her she'd take him for a trip to Rio,

near Rio, the town of Coelho da Rocha, in the state of
Rio. And she took him. When he was almost there, when
he could see Rio, he was watching, there were these
mountains all lit up, that kind of thing, totally different
from Cocotá. And he kept watching, one light was one
color, another another color, he'd never seen that before,
red, blue, a string of lights. And he kept looking at everything. "Im going to do that kind of work, nothing but that,
that very kind of work!" He always liked electricity,
that was when he began to look at the lights and that kind
of thing. So they arrived at night, at four in the morning,
he was watching everything, right? Never sleeping so he
wouldn't miss anything. Normally to this day he travels
an entire day on the bus, a whole night, and he won't
sleep for anything in the world so he can see the new
things that keep springing up, right? The aunt brought
him there and he stayed. Even though what he wanted to
do was turn around and go right back, even if he had to
walk. He wanted to go back but the aunt never gave him
the opportunity, she didn't give him any money, she didn't
let him go out, is that clear? And he even went hungry
in the aunt's house. She was a Bible woman, to this day
food is rationed in those people's houses. She was a be-
liever, of the Assembly of God. So food was really
rationed and he was always hungry. He was used to the
countryside, to having enough to eat, right? So he'd get
this little plate of food, really tiny, he'd say, "Aunt! . . .
no, it's nothing . . ." Because he was never one to complain, was he? Things were the way they were, later he'd
go out and buy homemade bread, one of those big round

loaves, he'd eat that and something else. That's why to this day he can't eat bread. The aunt would see him and tell him he had to eat his dinner and not so much bread, and he'd say yes, she was right, "Yes, aunty, it's all right." And he lived with her for five years, counting every hour because that was one hour less before he could go back and give Doña Carminha a big hug. But he swore he wouldn't go back unless it was in his own car. And he began to work as a mason, a mason's apprentice, because he didn't know anything about electricity. And by the time he was sixteen years old he couldn't stand not going back any longer.

—She certainly could stand not seeing you, she'd totally forgotten her third child by then.

She saw a lot of dust rising off the road that goes by the farm, they were planting something with her oldest daughter, planting lettuce, "What is that, girl? Is it a storm?" "No, ma'am, it's a car coming, a Maverick." "Who is it, girl?" "I don't know, ma'am, from this distance I can't see his face, but he has new clothes and I can smell his perfume already, very good perfume, even better than the kind from the plant that gives water," "Girl, he's going to laugh at us because we're poor, don't you think?" "I don't know, ma'am, that young man is going so fast, as for stopping here, he won't even think of it."

Chapter Three

He looked at himself in the mirror in the bar, long hair
down to his shoulders, beard, a hip guy, very fashionable, decked out, going wherever he pleased. He came to
Cocotá from far away, after a long trip. And that same
day he saw her go by, he noted the hour well on his wristwatch, gold colored, and mesh, too, but just plated. She
looked at the watch, not many had one in that town.

—Let's go, out of this bed! It's time to go to work. And
it's almost a two hour trip to downtown Rio.

He went after her right away, he whistled—pssht! She
looked and stuff like that, he whistled again, but she was
very young, she got scared, she left just like that, walking
very fast. And she disappeared. She went home and all
that. Back then his dream was to own a car, around that

time he'd bought a Gordini, it was the car of the day, one
of those low cars, you could say. He bought a Gordini
back then for a few bucks, you know? That's how he arrived, in that car, right? After years away from home,
bearded, long hair, his hair was really long. The mother
didn't recognize him. He arrived, banged his fist on the
front door of the house, of his mother's farm, so she said,
"The situation is as follows: I have a son by that name,
Josemar, but I don't know who you are." Then she went
to look for the daughters. They came and afterward he
stayed and talked alone with the mother for an hour and
a half, more or less, to see if she would recognize him,
but she didn't. She hadn't seen him since he'd left with an
aunt to begin his life of struggle and so on. But there he
was now, wasn't he? and she didn't recognize him at all.
So he showed her a snapshot. "Don't you remember this
snapshot, ma'am?" "Oh, yes, sir, now I remember, you
are my son." And he said, "You see what I mean! You
see what I mean, don't you? It's incredible, old lady, you
heartless old thing, but I forgive you," he said, and the
mother hugged him, kissed him and hung from his neck.

—Enough! Get up and go to work! Your mother this,
your mother that, it's not as if you're still a baby.

But by then he'd already seen that little girl, María da
Gloria, on the street; that was when he went after her, he
went up to the barber who cut his hair, who gave him
daily massages and all the things you have to do to yourself, it's the point of arrival, that barber shop, every time
he's back in town, so he arrived, she went by and he
asked, "Who is that precious thing?" And the barber,

"That's María da Gloria Rossi, Pino's daughter," that
kind of stuff, right? She was just a kid but she was already developed, almost twelve years old, a very strong
girl already, first rate, big boobs already. Very long
blond hair, white flesh, cheeks red with blood that was
heating up already, one day it was going to boil—and
spill all over? And he said to her, "Miss, don't go, I have
something to talk to you about." She laughed, sort of
embarrassed, and he insisting, or not? That's when she
moved away with three or four friends. "Shit on life!
What can I do now?" he asked the barber. "What can I do
to see her again?" "All you have to do is show up at the
square around seven-thirty, eight at night, she's generally
walking around the park, maybe she liked you right off,
then she'll open up to you like a parachute." So all
right, then. And he went back to the farm. "Now that
you're a long-hair, an unbelievable playboy, you'll knock
'em all dead," the barber said. By that time in the afternoon he'd given himself a good shave, combed his hair,
he looked a little more like the snapshot, right? And so
around six-thirty she was the first female he saw in the
park. She was walking around, all by herself, she sat on
a bench, he strolled over to that side, right? He kept insisting, even though generally no sooner would he head
her way than she'd run, she'd take off, she was afraid her
parents would see them, that whole business. He said to
himself, "Then what I have to do is the following: give
her time to send me a message." And he gave her time.
He went to a bar, had a beer, is that clear? Calmly, while
some of her friends showed up, she wrote a little note and

sent it to him, saying that she'd like to talk to him, but she's afraid of her parents, right? She'd like to talk to him, exchange a few words, but her parents might give her a beating. She sent someone to bring him the message. He read it, what you have to do in these cases. But the day was done and what the hell. Then he couldn't stand it anymore, "I have to get her to talk, shit! Does she go to school?" he asked the barber, who answered "She always goes by around eleven-thirty, that's the time." So at eleven-thirty the next day she was passing by. So he said, to himself, he talked to himself like a crazy person, "I'm going to go after her until I can talk to her as is only right, I want to hear her voice." So she spoke to him like this, "Hi!" she said when he appeared, right? And he, bang! He threw himself on her, he cornered her, "Baby, the business is as follows: I got your message and I think that a person's parents can't stop people from liking each other. My father, principally, isn't going to stop me, and I don't think yours will either. If that's what happens, if there's a problem I'll take it up with him, I'll tell him you're enjoying me. Why make a big fuss? What I want is for the two of us to talk and there won't be any problem, everything in order." And she said, "Would you have that much courage?" exactly those words. So he said, "Sure I have the courage, which one's your old man? I'll go find him." And she, "No! For the love of God don't do that!" And Thursday came, there was always music then in the park that was farthest away, he was there in the park, he remembers that day she had on a dress with white on the bottom and on top it was pink, the blouse. So here's how it was, he was fooling around with some other guys, fucking around a little. That was when they dedicated a song by Roberto Carlos, the guy said over the loudspeaker, "A young lady in pink and white dedicates this song to the boy with chestnut-colored hair, chestnut eyes, white skin, dressed all in white, black shoes and a wristwatch." In the park, the amusement park for juveniles, with swings and slides and all that. And that's how they began. They were making out, making out, and those things, secretly, right? at the exit of the school.

—There was a main park and another one that was more secluded.

—One is round, with a lot of plants and the fountain with jets of water shooting into the air, lots of fluorescent lights from underneath, which weren't there when he was small, an unbelievable park. That's the main one, the second park is the one right across from the gymnasium where she had to go for her physical-education classes, the street all around it is paved, roses, a lot of fountains, a very pretty lake, a lot of plants in that more secluded park, isn't that right? The river passes through on the other side, the Cocotá river, big as can be. Very pretty, full of trees and things like that, and the gymnasium is a gymnasium that is very pretty, well equipped, completely modern, right? Back then it was very modern, now it's not so much. So he lived, how would you say? on the prowl. OK. She lived about two kilometers from the gymnasium, they had to pass by the movie theater, by the two clubs, the main streets of the town, packed with houses, pharmacies, markets, stores,

many, she got through it all, no problem, and he always
following behind her right?

—Did you walk behind me or next to me?

Sometimes behind, sometimes next to her. At first behind, later he began to walk next to her when she felt
closer to him as a person, "The situation is as follows:
don't walk so fast, I feel like looking at you." And they
began to see each other when she had to go to that gymnasium stuff, already it was dark night, hidden, in that
very dark corner of the street. She'd leave the house and
go straight to see him. She'd get there crazy with excitement. Even though she didn't have her exercise class.

—You look bad in the mirror, tired, you didn't sleep
well, why did you keep waking up all night?

He slept badly last night. He'd sleep, wake up, go back
to sleep and wake up again, thinking, this is what happens sometimes, right? when he finishes these damned
construction jobs he began he'll be a little more relaxed
won't he? And have time for other things, not the same
old shit. He gave a woman an estimate for a new bathroom in an old apartment and when he tore down the wall
a pipe turned up that he didn't know was there, the pipe
broke and now the estimate is higher, but the owner
doesn't want to pay. And in the other building it was even
worse, where they made a window bigger, he and his
assistant, but they didn't have permission from the own-
ers of the apartment, and the superintendent of the building complained and said, "How can someone who's been
working at this for so long forget to get the required permission?" And when he gave the window estimate, materials cost one thing and now they cost something else,

fucking inflation, it ends up with him having to dig into his own pocket. And the mother is sick, if she doesn't get well she has to see another doctor, and if she doesn't get well she has to have another treatment, even more expensive, and the only thing she has to sell is this house. He slept badly all night and now he has to go to work.

—If you didn't have to work you could stay in bed and try to rest.

If he fell asleep he'd wake up again, because he's worried.

—But it would be good for you to rest at least an hour longer, in peace.

That woman with the old apartment is waiting with a flooded bathroom and a broken pipe.

—You could tell her that the bus was stopped for an hour on the road.

He wakes up at night and thinks that to finish the fucking jobs he'll have to dig into his own pocket.

—You don't think about the last time we saw each other because that makes you feel bad too, right?

She told her parents she was going to some cousins' house, she had loads of relatives around there, right? and that type of thing. And when she showed up one day he said to her, "I won't put up with this any longer, if you're ready to lay your cards on the table so everything's out in the open, nothing secret from your mother and father, you have nothing to worry about, because I'm going to go up and talk to them." Then one day she pointed him out to her mother, she passed by holding her mother's arm and pointed him out, "It's that boy over there." Then the mother poked her with her elbow and he noticed and the old lady smiled, and he said to himself, like a crazy person, "Hell! Now that the mother looked at me and smiled, everything's in order, right?" If the bitch hadn't liked him she would have made a bad face, right? That was when she passed by with the mother but they didn't turn their heads. They disappeared, he lost sight of them. But he stayed on guard there, is that clear? Because they had to go by another time, on the way home, so right then, when it was getting close to ten at night, the town was already pretty deserted, the two showed up around there again. He said to himself, "What the fuck, I'll walk over there and approach them."

—Where could we have been, me and my mother?"

They'd been to visit one of her uncles who was sick on another street that he didn't even know, right? Back then he never took those streets with the best houses. She was coming with her mother, he was waiting wasn't he? The car was parked, he was next to it, the radio of the Maverick was on, and he said, "Hey, I'm going to approach them!" Thinking only about that, "I'm going to approach them, I'm not going to sweat it any longer, if they get mad, tough luck and if they don't get mad, perfect." So when he went right in front of her she got all scared and grabbed onto the mother's arm, she was afraid he was going to approach them, wasn't she? And he did approach them, "Good evening, ma'am, how are you?" He spoke to the mother herself, and he held out his hand, and he worked himself up to make the introduction himself, "Josemar at your service." It was close to a month and a half now, about that, that they'd been seeing each other, but he really liked the daughter, and he wanted to make it very clear that he'd already been talking to her and he wanted absolutely nothing muddy, "Ma'am, your daughter is still very young, but see how she wears her hair long already, like a young lady, she's already grown up and has hair as pretty as her mother's, I see that now. I am also a young boy, but I'm very intelligent and later in the future you can be my mother-in-law and I'll be your son-in-law, everything in order." There he was saying that to the mother, and the mother believing all of it.

—Did you like my mother?

He liked her a lot, he was crazy about her. The mother told him, "OK, don't worry, I'm listening, I'm beginning to understand, but as far as my husband's concerned, I never saw a thing." And the daughter was watching her, "But the day I see you together I'm going to give this one a few lashes of the whip." She said she was going to hit her with a whip. It was only a joke, because her mother was really good, "No, the situation is as follows: I told you that as far as I'm concerned there's no problem. The problem is her father. So you can go out, meet around here, hidden from her father. It's all I can do for my pretty little daughter who I love so much," the mother told him. "Then it's this way," he said, "since you permit it, ma'am, would it be possible for me to go up to your husband, who is the father in this case, and talk to him?" "No," she answered, she didn't think so, "because he's pretty bad tempered, he could say no, and even do something brutal to you, son." A few days went by and he didn't see María da Gloria, until she showed up at the door of the gymnasium and she'd had her hair cut, "My mother made me cut it like the other girls my age." And at that stage of things the soccer business came up, the next Sunday there was an important game. So he signed up for the team to decide the championship, and the old man was one of the coaches on the team, her father, right? He'd give his life, if necessary, for his team. And then, fuck them, they put up a notice, "Today Josemar Ferreira debuts," on the Cocotá Sports Club's soccer team. And the public didn't know him back then, he'd spent his childhood there but he'd left many years ago. He trained on Wednesday and Thursday and Sunday, he was going to be thrown onto the starting team.

—That's not true. They didn't let people from the farms join the town team.

It was their opinion that he was an excellent athlete. It seemed to them that he was one of the best athletes who'd ever been in that town, on that team. So he told them he'd spent his life playing on one team or another. So her father, her own father, told him the following, he still didn't know anything at the time, but then he headed over to him and said, "You play nice and open, left side, right at the edge of the field, personally I like my forwards like that, you have the characteristics I like in soccer." But the old man didn't know that the daughter was seeing someone, he still didn't know. So when the new guy began to play on the team, the people who had seen him following her to the gymnasium and to the house and talking with her around those parts, the people, when he got the ball, they yelled, "That's the son-in-law of old man Rossi, the team coach." So, fuck it, the guy begins to see red, "Hell! Is it possible that this guy is hanging around my daughter and I don't know anything about it." And this and that. So by the time the game ended that day he'd made three goals, on that day, he was the crack player of the very team, right? Then, hell, that's old man Rossi's son-in-law, the whole crowd was saying it. So the old man went to find out about it, so when night fell, after soccer and stuff, everybody came to embrace him, and all the public, all the people there in the bar went up to the best player, "I don't know if you saw that the people were making fun of me, saying that you're my son-in-law, and I don't know what else." The old man didn't know that the crack player had already been talking to his daughter for quite a while. There was the opportunity to tell him, really face to face, "Oooh . . . but your daughter, what does she look like? Would she be perhaps the little blond with the little gold loop earrings, very tiny like the ones infants wear?" The old man said, "She's blond, she used to have long hair and now they've cut it." And, "Look sir," he answered, "I'm going to be frank with you: I am, I am really in love with your daughter, I love her with all my soul, she's a really excellent girl." He said that, to the father himself. And the father, "Oh, thank you very much!" and stuff like that, he gave him a strong handshake, that kind of thing, and he couldn't work up the courage, but he wanted to give him one of those real hugs, and a very strong kiss on the forehead, hug the old man hard, until his ribs cracked a little, even though the old man was stronger than shit, Italian from hell, but he held out his hand and the old man didn't refuse it. Everything in order, then, "Now you'll stay on the team, and also, if I'm not mistaken, maybe now you'll stay in town, right?" And he said, "As long as I can, depending on conditions," he told him, "because I like your daughter and you're one of the directors of the club." "Let's say it's all settled, right?" the father said, and he said, "Oh, perfect! I didn't come to this town to make money, I want to play soccer because my father lives here, you're a friend of my father's, isn't that true, you were always a friend of my father's, weren't you?" Because his father is Astolfo, who works on the farm, married to Doña Carminha—but please don't go and believe what they say! Because he's whiter they say he isn't really his father's son.

—Don't talk about that to my father, our elders know more.

The crack player will talk about whatever he wants to, and if the fucking old guy gives him any shit he'll just floor him with one blow.

—Don't get mad like that—do you know something? I'd never seen as handsome a young man and with hair so long.

He arrived from Rio in '69, and in that fucking town no one had let their hair grow long yet.

—The rancher, the landowner was the handsomest man I'd ever seen in my life, a man with no gray hair, he didn't wear his hair long, he had a white hat with a wide brim.

But later she saw him, in the park, he turned into the crack of the team, the best player in the club. She began to like the young man.

—Yes. Because the young man looked a lot like the landowner.

She began to like the young man and that's all there is to it. Later that afternoon after the soccer game, everyone was happy with life, he and her father, but one time they all went to the farm of some of her father's friends, everyone went. Everyone on foot on the road, to the party, to drink a little, a good beer, passing by those farms all planted, those shrubs, he, she, her mother, the whole family, the father, the brothers, everyone in the world. It was the big family reunion, right? An unbelieveable reunion. That's what he remembers. That was in the beginning.

—Once you wanted to come with my family to the country but they wouldn't let you.

He asked her to let her hair grow again. At night in the country at the party, none of this suit and tie stuff, in the country it was all bermudas or shorts and not much else. But it was at night.

—And what could happen?

He liked them a lot, he was crazy about those parties, but at night you can't see very much and afterward people forget more easily, because they didn't see everything too clearly. It's harder to remember. That's why he took her to the country one morning, just the two of them, at home she told them she was going to school.

—I'm afraid of the country, there might be snakes, my father hears if one gets close.

He talked her into going by themselves, to look for birds. They love her, the little birds, because she treats them very well, right? She puts a lot of food in the cage, then when they're set free after two weeks, everything in order, they come back to the cage. A little bird knows when you treat it well. And she used to take good care of the plants, too, she watered them early in the morning, before the sun came out, because the sun overheats them and without water they dry out. And she also liked horses even though they bucked, she loved them, she rode them right, she'd even take a good fall and scratch her face a little. But animals loved her.

—None of the animals was bad with me?

The cows, they don't like women or little ones. A cow has only to set eyes on a woman and wants to knock her over and then stomp on her. She didn't like wild cows either, she'd see a cow and she'd take off, she'd run like crazy.

—And the male animals? None of them was bad with me?

None that he can remember. The only male animal around there was him. And yes, he was bad with her.

—Why?

He wanted to mount her, without mercy. And even if the female repents afterward, it's too late, she's got to enjoy it and she's lost, she waits for the male to come back and mount her again.

—No, you weren't bad with me, that's not true.

Yes he was bad! Hell! And once he got her real used
to it, afterward he'd keep her waiting, because he knew
she had no choice but to sit and wait for him to come and
mount her, anytime he chose. After he was with his other
females. He always had loads of women, is that clear?
Single ones, married ones, whatever he wanted. Among
themselves they never found out what was happening, but
they suspected, and he stepped hard on the accelerator,
they were begging for it, and he'd go full blast, until he
made them jump from pleasure and pain.

—I don't remember that pleasure or that pain. But I
remember that when the landowner passed my house he
took off his hat to greet me and then I kept thinking that
you were even handsomer than he was. And I wanted to
give you a hat so you could take it off as you passed my
house, to greet the whole family.

They brought a bedspread, they brought everything,
pillows, to the countryside. To spend the whole day in
the thicket, right? It was going to be really unbelievable,
no one would be able to see them. But there they were far
away, almost no one passed that way. They'd go into the
grove and no one would be able to see them anymore,
they'd disappear forever. There are a lot of groves. He
even passed by that place a little while ago, last time he
went to Cocotá. It had already been a long time that
they'd been going together, it had been more or less a
year they'd spent talking. Including her mother, this last
time, "Just think how long you were going together,
right? From the moment you left her and left town everything changed in this house." The mother told him that

everything changed for them after he disappeared, right? The mother doesn't go out anymore, she doesn't go out in the streets, she stays inside watching over the daughter. Because the daughter does the same thing, she goes to church now, she's always in church, that kind of thing, is that clear? Praying that she doesn't have an attack, and she starts scratching the walls with her fingernails, from nerves. She doesn't go out anymore, she doesn't go to the dances, she doesn't go to parties, she doesn't go to anything anymore.

—But that day I went to the country instead of school, true or not?

They had been together the whole day, it was getting close to nightfall, sprawled on the grass. It was as follows: they'd had a fight earlier, and he told her if she didn't give him what he asked for he'd never see her again, she was between a rock and a hard place, "What will it be like?" she wanted to know, and he told her, "I'll tell you about it." And he pried her open very slowly, because it was a tough little cherry.

—It was there that it finally happened, in the thicket?

Son of a bitch! That wasn't soft, no, he hurt himself, even, and he hurt her. There in the thicket. After that they stopped. So about five days later they started up again, always in the open countryside.

—The first time, was it really in the thicket?

He convinced her to go to the countryside alone. Shit! He certainly had waited long, fuck it, but at last they were out there alone, weren't they? At home she said she was going to school, as every morning.

—Where is it that we're going? What will that pain be like? I don't know what it's like.

He told her, "I'll tell you about it when we get there, you'll be able to pick lots of flowers." She liked flowers so much! Roses, daisies, dahlias, sunflowers, the bigger the sunflower, the better.

—What did I do with the flowers?

Generally she put them in a jar on top of some table, on the bed table, too, he imagines, next to the television set. She asked him, "Why is it I like them so much?" And he, "I never knew, those are women's mysteries, women generally like that kind of thing, like flowers."

—Why do women like them more than men do?

They're pretty, people pass by and see some plants and say, "Look how well those plants are doing, and they're flowering!" Then generally things go well, everybody is happy and goes about his business—the enemies are hummingbirds and bees. Bees generally open flowers to take out the honey and the hummingbird does too. It eats the flower, mounts it really well. They suck the juice out. The flower dies—if it was going to last ten days, it lasts three or four, doesn't it? In general terms they suck the flower and leave it with nothing left inside. The flowers' friends are the sun, a little in the morning, and water. If it's a flower from a houseplant the women are the ones who water it every day. If it's a flower from the thicket it has to wait for the morning dew, right? His car, when he had one, shone all wet like that, from the morning dew.

Chapter Four

—You went back to sleep. You woke up a little while ago but you didn't listen to me.

He always asked her to grab him hard with one hand.

—Enough! Stop feeling around.

And she always did what he wanted, even in her own house, she'd always grab it, she'd squeeze it hard, that winner, right? So then he'd move his hand really hard over those big boobs of hers, he'd rub them well, he'd give her an overall massage, she'd go crazy, she'd get to the point where she was almost in tears, crazy with excitement, she'd even yell. She'd make noises like this, "Ooooh, aaaah, ummm, ooooh. Oh, how nice! My boy-friend is so good to me." She couldn't help saying all that.

—That's all true, but it happened a long time ago and times change, we have to talk about other things.

She'd stick her hand down his pants and take everything out. She had to suck, too, right? But she never did that. She'd say no. He always said to her, "What would it cost you to suck it a little?" And that kind of thing, "That's a part of love." "No, no, I won't do that." She wouldn't accept it for anything in the world. She never even gave it a kiss, "Give the little pink club a kiss." She kissed the boyfriend's mouth a lot, but she never kissed the club. She said no, "The woman doesn't do that." Now, right? Maybe if it were now, maybe she'd do it. Because now a woman likes to suck a club. Times change. She believed in him a lot, because he told her he was going to marry her, so she wouldn't have that doubt, "Do you believe everything I'm telling you, my love?" She was well on her way to putting out, yes? She'd tell him, "What do I have to do so you see I believe you?" And things like that. And he, "The situation is as follows: I'm not God, for you to believe in me, you'd better believe in God and not in me." That's what he always told her. And she said to him, "But . . ." And that stuff, because she felt that life was changing, she was passing from childhood into being a young woman. So she acted crazy, at that time of life they go crazy, demented, yes? And they give what they have to the guy they really love. So back then, he was waiting for her phase, when the phase came up he felt that she was in that phase and he attacked, yes? The important thing was that that day in the country Delfina didn't go with the two of them.

—Who was she?

Her best friend, she was more grown up already, slier, the one who always brought him the little notes when Gloria couldn't come. One of her very best friends, later she became a robber friend. Because she wanted to rob Gloria, she even propositioned him, "I'll give you what she's too young for and can't give you."

—Your mother left for the hospital before six this morning, she could be back any minute now and find you still in bed. My papa was right in all the bad things he said about you. This is the last time I'm asking you to get up.

He wants to stay in bed just a few more minutes, that's all, right? Because something else he shouldn't forget is that he taught María da Gloria to look at the moon, which before she never thought you could look at for a long time. He knew how to do that, someone taught him.

—Who?

He never told María da Gloria so she wouldn't get mad. In the country during the day she did look at birds. He told her she should also look at the clouds in the sky, right? And during the day at that nice green, that countryside, many different things, a lot of pretty rocks.

—You're still not up! I don't want to hear another word.

Tall rocks, big ones, right? Then they'd run to see who could catch the other, so usually he'd hide behind those

huge pieces of rock, well hidden, and she'd start following him around, like he used to do to her. He told
her, "You have to shut your eyes, cover your eyes with
your hands, and then you can start looking for the one
who's hiding." So he'd quickly hide in the thicket and
behind those huge fucking rocks, and these were the
things they used to do to be happy, games and things
like that, right? He was hard to find, and if she didn't
find him he'd turn up. "Here I am!" and that stuff. And
she'd go running, then she'd say, "Oh this guy! He
knows how to hide so well!" So generally when she tried
to hide he'd find her. She'd say, "Enough is enough!
Now I'm the one who's going to hide." And he'd agree.
And the rocks around there were generally black, dark,
with white streaks, some very pretty rocks could be found
around that area, and hills, very big trees, lots of different things, plenty of wildflowers and wood from Ipê,
very nice, mahogany, things of that sort. Would she
remember that? Or doesn't she think about him anymore?

— . . .

There were a lot of wildflowers, yellow ones, very
pretty. They stand for the colors of Brazil, right? The
leaves of the plants are green, the Brazilian flag, and
those strips of white rock make the Brazilian stars. He
doesn't like the color yellow for clothes, but he likes
yellow flowers a lot. Let's say he went into a store where
they sell clothes, he'd never buy anything in yellow. And
sometimes she would ask him why he never put on anything yellow. She never wore that color either, she'd

promised him, is she wearing yellow nowadays? Why isn't she thinking about him at this moment?

— . . .

To him, yellow stands for a lot of things right? Little yellow birds, cannaries, and flowers, he likes seeing that color. Then the two of them—right—they had a lot of fun, they roamed around aimlessly, nothing to do, all they had to think about was whether to climb one hill or another, a higher one, is that clear? Personally he doesn't like yellow or red clothes, he doesn't like red shirts or red pants, he'd never wear them. One day she told him she'd figured out why he didn't like yellow clothes or very bright red, but now he can't remember what it was.

— . . .

He likes to see those colors, when people give red roses it stands for a lot of affection from one friend to another, from one girlfriend to another or from a man to a woman. He likes getting it as a gift, isn't that true?

— . . .

And another thing he likes that's red is jelly, he doesn't like sweet things too much, but he does eat jelly once in awhile, because he's funny about eating, there isn't much he likes. And he hates seeing blood, he doesn't like it at all, it drives him crazy, he hates seeing blood. A co-worker on the construction project was wounded, a brick fell on him from six meters, he was desperate when he saw the face all red with blood. He had to take him to the hospital and stay with him all day. And when he saw her bleeding, he didn't like it at all, either, frankly, it upset him, right? What could she be

thinking about now? She's not thinking about him because the parents spoke badly of him.

— . . .

He didn't get a kick out of it, he doesn't like any kind
of blood. It could be the most beautiful woman in the
world, if she starts bleeding near him he feels sick.
Everything, he doesn't even like a steak if it has bloody
streaks. He's against blood, a hundred percent. Just
talking about blood he feels sick already. Sometimes she
cut pink roses for him, not completely red.

— . . .

He had a lot of girlfriends and he was very well loved,
and generally he remembers the pink roses he'd get,
generally when he was so popular with that group of
little girls who were all friends with each other, right?
He'd get a lot of roses, but later, now he doesn't get many
roses because he doesn't live with that group he lived
with in the old days, is that clear? So there's no way to
get roses and that kind of thing. These days on his birthday he works like any other day. Doesn't she remember
his birthday? At this moment she isn't thinking about
him, she's not going shopping, not even to the park. She
doesn't leave the house, she lies sprawled on the bed
getting sadder every minute. Like him, sprawled on the
bed.

— . . .

He doesn't have many friends where he lives. And
generally the friends he has aren't good ones, right?
It's not worth anything like that. They're friends who
want money, they want him to buy them drinks, and he

won't put up with that business, is that clear? He tries to stick to himself and his black brother, they're the only ones who understand each other. Because you can't always be alone right? What could María da Gloria be doing right now? He'd better get out of this fucking bed, right?

— . . .

The truth is he doesn't have a black brother, that one was just an orphan, he saw him the day they brought him home. He took care of him and a snake never bit him, because he took care of him and taught him to listen when one approached. They don't all make noise, the wildest one makes noise, the golden surucucu, the prettiest snake of all, it has a rattle, so when it hears a person a kilometer away it begins to shake it, it does this, Tic, tic-tic-tic. It makes a noise with its snout, stirring the poison around in its snout. The bite of that snake is incredible, if it bites someone he dies five minutes later. So when it goes to attack it breathes heavily, it breathes furiously with the urge to bite someone. It used to scare Gloria when he'd talk about snakes, right? She'd cover her ears, isn't that true?

— . . .

Once he saw a dog, right? The snake bit it, it took less than three seconds to die, one minute he heard it spring, and the next minute it bit. The dog tried to bite it, it tried this, it tried that, the snake succeeded in fastening onto it and the dog fell, the other one kept biting it, gnawing on it all over. Because to live happily it has to inject the poison into the prey. Which can only come out by biting, right? If it bites it stays well for a long time, if it doesn't bite then the poison starts to make the fucking snake sick, it screws it up for a long time, it gets upset, full of the urge to fasten on to someone, to get rid of the poison. So once it gets someone, it bites him all it wants, it bites him as much as it can, it winds itself around the person and bites and gnaws all over, right? It bites whatever animal gets within reach, whatever shows up—dog, monkey, whatever presents itself—but with a guy it's harder because he hears the uproar, a sharp guy like him, and the guy runs. He left Cocotá just in time, right? They wanted to throw a lasso around his neck. But he escaped. And all they're left with is that sad house with a daughter more upset than I don't know what. And if she isn't thinking about him she can go to hell.

— . . .

It happened to him several times, he heard it, once he was hunting birds with the shotgun, hunting juritis, a bird as big as a chicken, to eat. He was whistling, absentmindedly, he was under the shade of some big rocks, he looked up and saw a huge snake. Going across. He whistled the way the juritis whistle, but it was a snake and it whistled too. He said to himself, "Son of a fucking bitch!" He'd been looking for a bird and he'd found that shit whore, so he moved back and she was coming down on top of him with that mouth open, the only thing he could do was aim the shotgun well and fire. When he fired it fell right on top of him, but it was already dying. He happily pulled the trigger right there, bam! The whore fell, but another time it was incredible, he was eating something on top of some rocks, right? and he saw one far away, very thick, his arms almost wouldn't go around it, more than 20 meters long. So he stayed there and watched it the whole time, he watched it for like five hours, not doing anything else, generally she'd move along, slide along, all that, until she went into a hole in the ground nearby. She disappeared. "Shit, that snake's big as hell!" And his idea was to put out a big hook, to catch it. He'd put out a piece of meat on a hook like for fishing, yes? and a really strong cord, and he'd start to pull it, no? that big snake choking. He had it all set up but at a point forgot what he was supposed to do next and he called the father at the moment the big snake stuck out its head, "Virgin Saint, let's get a move on, son, this slimy beast is a monster, right?" So they ran away and later the father went to look for who knows how many liters of burning alcohol and he tossed it down the hole and lit a fire, and so inside the rocks there was rolling around that you could hear. Under the earth, crazy to get out, but it couldn't. No one knows if it died or what happened to it, if it went crazy from rage, it can fuck itself, the son of a bitch. Roast in hell! But since then he never saw it again. When he'd talk about snakes María da Gloria would go running, so she wouldn't listen, how many years ago is that? No matter how much he wants to remember, sometimes he even forgets her face. Her mouth.

— . . .

He wanted to see the snake free, is that clear? He'd
seen it free more than once, but he couldn't get close to
it, the closest was one or two hundred meters, but when
it heard someone close by it got all excited, it raised it's
head a meter and a half, two meters, to find the person.
Then he'd hide but he wouldn't lose sight of it, although
with the slightest movement he'd take off like a shot. His
father would hear when one was getting close. Now he's
not there, the father gave up working, he quit, he lost
hope and quit working. But he's old now. A long time
ago he also let everything go to hell, and so each of them
had to work things out for himself as best he could.
The father used to work nonstop, until he lost hope, he
saw that work doesn't pay and he declared a strike, a
strike against himself, right? He didn't do anything anymore, he went to the bar and had some beers, the wife
stayed home with the children who were starting to grow
up. She did the following: she went around and sold
whatever they had, so as not to see the brood in that
position. She sold the hogs, the hens, the goats, and
brought home whatever she could, and on top of that she
still paid his debts, is that clear? It wasn't easy. María
da Gloria doesn't know what it is to go hungry. If she
went hungry for one day her goddamn nerves would disappear, fuck.

— . . .

They didn't even have one hen left, or a goat—nothing
but nothing—then his mother started washing other
people's clothes, but it wasn't enough, and then she went

as a servant to a house, that one time only, right? No shame in that, to feed the children.

— . . .

His mother had four back then, right? Nowadays the father's changed, he's changed completely, he doesn't hit the bottle anymore. But she showed up at that house and asked them to let her clean everything, but would they pay her something in advance because the children didn't have anything to eat that day. Those people were acquaintances of hers, and better-off, they'd help her out once in a while. There was nothing to worry about because she sent the groceries home, and she stayed to work, but it didn't matter because now there was something to eat on the farm so that his sister could cook dinner for everyone, right? The mother washed, cleaned, all day away from home, she weeded the vegetable gardens of those houses. That's why now she can't stand on her feet, poor old lady, she sold the chickens and then their last goat young and tender, a kid, to buy other things to eat, but once they couldn't sell that goat, they killed it and the brood ate it, right? and it's delicious, young goat meat, even now he gets cravings for it, it's incredible, and tonight there'll be a dish of rice because the mother always has something to eat even if it's almost the end of the month. He could eat a steak, even more than goat meat.

— . . .

His mother never abandoned them. And she'll never let him go without a roof over his head. She'd let them kill her first.

— . . .

And she didn't get back from the hospital before he left for work. She didn't see that he'd stayed in bed like two hours longer. When he gets off that fucking train at night the mother's going to say, "Such a long day at work, my son!" And he's going to tell her the truth, that today again the fare to Rio went up. She would make that porridge and those soups. She'd take turnips and cook them with rice, this was back then, of course. There was never any meat, no money for that, she'd make a special polenta that she made, and it was good enough to lick your fingers. She takes corn flour, seasons it with red pepper, puts in some chicory, cuts the leaves in strips and mixes it, and it makes a son-of-a-bitch of a soup, a thick soup, really unbelievable. He still asks her to make it, he says the following, "Ma'am, make that soup that you made when we were broke. . . ." And so she says, "OK, but I don't like to think about those times, my son." He says, "Don't give me a hard time, just make it because I like it." And she makes it, right? Polenta, peppers, chicory, all mixed together, she throws it into a casserole and it makes a heap of food. All boiled, right? The only thing is that it doesn't have any meat or anything, just polenta, turnips, and the chicory leaves. Nowadays, she also makes a lot of rice for the son, with fried banana and a good steak. Tonight even though nobody has told him he already knows there won't be any polenta, just rice, "Son, from now to the end of the month there isn't enough for anything else, and if I don't get stronger the only thing left to do will be what I never wanted to do . . ." He doesn't listen to her when she starts with that.

— . . .

If the mother leaves, Zilmar can come and live with him. One morning there was a little black child in the house across the street from María da Gloria's, the mother was a servant and she'd died, "Won't you take it home with you, Carminha, to raise with all your children? We'll give you some cruzeiros and this way all of us are saving his life, right?" In that house full of rich people they had one daughter, Olga.

— . . .

Olga spied on them from her window when he and Gloria did their business in the dark. His mother used to stop by Olga's house every day to say hello. He'd go, too, and played with Olga until it got dark for the other business, across the street. And when his mother went back to work on the farm she started having children again, he was very small, "Josemar! Josemar!" his father would always call him, like a screw, he tightened it a little more each time until he was stuck, he couldn't move anymore. And sometimes the mother couldn't defend him because she was sick in bed or sometimes she was about to give birth. And if she was about to give birth she didn't go to work anywhere else, but she washed and ironed for other people there at home. Tonight when he gets back if the mother's health is better he'll give her a big hug, "Very good, ma'am, congratulations, you're getting better, and quickly! Right? Or aren't you getting any better?"

— . . .

He went and told the mother that the father was turning the screw tighter every time, but she was in bed complaining about pains, because she was with child again. She wasn't to blame, right? She was feeling very bad.

— . . .

He said to her, "Ma'am, ma'am! Please, when will you be well again? Ma'am, I'm so tired I can't go on, I rounded up the cows, already, weeded the ground for the tomatoes, I pulled out the poison grass, now he's going to send me to cut the cane, and my arms hurt, and I have a sore on this hand!" Mama! Where is she? Did they take her to the hospital already to have a baby?

— . . .

There was a school in the countryside. There was one in town and one in the country. He went to the one in the country and the teacher was named Valsei. He liked her, he'd always go home thinking about her, right? He never expected to know her so well one day, right? She lived in town and he lived in the country. She was single, that teacher, and never missed class, she was never sick. She didn't do outside washing and ironing. So he went there to learn from this very pretty teacher. He liked her, but with that crazy puppy love. He wrote her a note and put it under her attendance book. He was eleven years old already, he still hadn't learned to write well, what was it he wrote her? "My dear teacher Valseí: I know I respect your presence, not only because you're a great teacher, but I'm crazy in love with you. I know that by doing this I could damage my studies and get a terrible punishment." Also it was hard for her when she saw it to believe it. It took months before she talked to him about the business, he was always expecting a reaction, back then, is that clear? So one day, everything was going great, she spoke to him, it's that when she read the note she thought it was childish, right? "I don't know who wrote me this note." So back then when teachers wanted to get a student's attention so it wasn't in front of the others she made him wait until everyone left the classroom. After class she'd make the kid kneel on the prickly corn. She'd throw the corn on the floor and you had to kneel there to repent. That day he stood still, thinking she would hit him, because back then teachers hit. She took a handful of corn and was slowly sprinkling it on the floor, and she asked him if he had other brothers and sisters. He told her he was the third child, and later there were more because those were better times and now the mother had had another after a long time, and she was expecting another one, because the father was working on the farm again and they had enough to eat, "Miss, the situation is as follows: I'm the one who sent you that little message, I really think that to tell the truth is to feel, to let my feelings out into the open, that's nothing unusual." Then he said to her that, all right, he loved her. He spoke frankly, quite frankly, "You don't have to worry, you can make me kneel on prickly corn, you can hit me, but you won't convince me. I'm completely crazy about you, I'm in love. I'm going crazy with desire to kiss you on the lips," he said to her, and she smiled at him and let out a laugh, and then said to him like this, "I called you over to give you some advice; this is going to hurt your studies, but I'm going to thank you for the courtesy of writing me that note, I liked it, you were the first student who ever lost his head over me, up to now I've had more than a thousand students and none of them ever told me they loved me." Then he said to her, "Look, dear teacher, the situation is as follows: I love you truly, I'm going to wait for you, when I grow up and I'm older I'm going to find you and become your boyfriend, is that clear?" So she said he had a lot of years to go but there were a lot of pretty things in the world, not only in Rio de Janeiro and São Paulo, but right there in the countryside, and that he had to look at how beautiful the plants were. And he said that at night he thought about her because everyone went to sleep early and the mother was always sprawled all over the bed after working all day, washing and ironing outside, and with child, while he'd get sad thinking about her, the teacher. And the teacher Valseí told him that at night you can't see the plants and the hills and the wildflowers, but you have to look at the moon and the clouds, which are very pretty, and the stars. "I seem pretty to you, and that's why at night you get sad and feel like seeing me, but there are many other things even prettier still and you have to learn to remember to go out and look at them, and that way your sadness will pass." Everyone slept on the farm, the father too, he wasn't going to the bar now to drink those beers, or to other parts even farther away, he was working in the countryside again. He'd sleep all night, even though he thought the third child wasn't his own.

— . . .

He treated the third child as if he were adopted. He wasn't jealous of another man, or suspicious, he didn't have that problem of thinking about somethink like, you know, something absurd, but generally he said stupid things, a pack of lies. He didn't say that the third child wasn't his, but he made jokes. He never got to the stage of ever speaking straight out, clearly, but the grandmother, the paternal one, the grandmother of the third once said it. That the third was the son of the landowner, who had a lot of land and that the father plowed it with a team of oxen. But the third knew this wasn't true because his mother was a very honest woman, very correct. It was only a joke that went around because the third was different from all the brothers and sisters. He was a lot whiter, but not too much, but his hair wasn't black and coarse like an Indian's, it was wavy and chestnut colored. Gloria always said that, right? "I think your hair is even softer than mine."

— . . .

The brothers and sisters all had coarse black hair, the mother had coarse black hair down to her waist, the father's hair was cut very short, and with that thought always, maybe that's why he asked more from him than from the others, right? "Josemar! Quick, weed the ground, all that soil up to where it ends, and then those sacks of pumpkins have to be brought in, and worst of all, what you hate to do most, which is cut the cane, scoundrel! Quick, cut the cane I told you!" The parents weren't Indians, they'd been born on some farm, or in town, but not in the thicket far away, nothing like that! What do people think? The parents' parents weren't either, but the grandparents of the parents, yes. The third child asked the maternal grandmother if she was Indian and she said no, her mother yes, they caught her in the thicket, deep in the jungle, they threw a lasso and that kind of thing, right? They caught her with a lasso, and then they tamed her, right? That was the information that was passed on to him, but the Indians around there weren't dangerous, they caught them and mastered them and little by little they became normal people, is that clear?

—They were savages, they shot arrows, they shot them at everyone.

No! They weren't dangerous! They attacked if they were attacked. If the daughter of an Indian man or an Indian woman was kidnapped, then they'd attack by any means, yes? With arrows, those kinds of things, clubs, in town there's a museum, with the feathers, everything for their heads, and their pots, clay, and those big smoking pipes. But in his grandmother's house they didn't have anything like that anymore, even though there are still Indians, in the jungle, but way in, very deep in the jungle, like two hundred miles, you can go but when you go into the jungle it's easy to get lost, and there deep in the jungle there are some plots of earth that are planted with grain, only what they need to eat in 1900,

and something the grandmother told him that they'd
caught that Indian girl, and they tamed her until she
turned into a normal woman, and she wore dresses,
clothes, because before she used to walk around with
that thing like a bikini, and the custom of praying. Because they had a lot of faith in God, right? Like his
mother, who's never done anything else in her life but
work for the children and believe in God like a saint.

— . . .

That one they brought from the thicket and tamed
later on still kept that up, the prayer of the descendants
of the Indians, when they're about to go to bed they make
a noise, they begin to pray when they go to sleep, right?
That's what they say in the family. She prayed in their
language, not in Portuguese. In his family they're sons
of sons of Indians, not one of them is Portuguese, completely pureblood, a purified blood, you could say, from
living honestly, every one of them with his work, and
from not having any Portuguese in the family. Or
Italian, either. But he has to get off at the next bus stop
and start working on that fucking mess of a bathroom.
Because if he didn't have anything to do he'd go back
to Santísimo on the first bus going that way, the mother
must be back from the hospital by now and there's no one
there to take care of her.

Chapter Five

—Please don't talk to me about snakes, there might be one close by and we're not seeing it.

If she's afraid, why does she get into this? He can defend himself, what does he need her for?

—It's three very dark blocks to the other bus station.

Today if they attack him they'll have something to steal, this super steak he's carrying home in a bag. But he can defend himself from snakes, what does she think? Even though in this fucking city they don't even have those. He'd often go to set traps to catch birds, right? And there he was, absentmindedly setting the trap, when he looked around, and some twenty centimeters from his shoulder was a green snake. The same as the leaves of those trees, completely green, but neither water snakes nor green snakes ever bite. No sir. They go running like a fart when they see someone, what they eat is rats, mosquitoes, insects, those little slimy ones. Wild snakes kill oxen and drink water in the river and swallow pigs whole, or hens. They attack with their tails as much as with their heads. They pierce you, they puncture you. Then they bite with their mouth, two teeth like two hooks, no one can get them off. Water snakes don't bite, and he and María da Gloria can go ahead and strip and take a bath in the river.

—No.

Snakes don't bite in the river because the poison dissolves in water. A snake doesn't drink water, not for anything in the world. Because when it's thirsty then it doesn't drink, they say it drinks every ten years or every six months. That's something he doesn't remember, but he does know that first it spits all the poison out onto a leaf, one of those with the round necks, like it was a washbasin. They shoot out all the poison. Later, when they're finished drinking water, they come back and suck it all up again, because when they don't have any food they feed on the poison.

—Don't talk to me about wild animals, they scare me. I know what happened this afternoon with that old man who asked you to do him a favor, to unclog the kitchen sink.

A hole covered on four sides, sealed with bricks, a snake fell in but can't get out, it doesn't have anything to eat, ten, fifteen years. It doesn't die. It lives off the poison. The thing is it gets thinner and thinner, the width of a piece of cord. But it doesn't die. He had a friend, a very young guy, and this happened there near Cocotá, who cornered a snake in a hole and covered it, he put a rock on top of it, and ten or fifteen years later he passed by and remembered, "Once I stuck a snake down that hole," a hole nearby. So he started digging and digging until he found it, but when he finished uncovering it he thought it would be dead already, right? And when he took the rock off, the snake came up behind him and bit his hand, he fell over dead right there. These things happen, the boy was eighteen or twenty years old. He doesn't remember the name of the dead boy, he was a friend of his.

—The old man who lives next door to the apartment with the broken bathtub is almost blind.

The old man called him to unclog the kitchen sink. He went in and saw that the old man was alone and couldn't see what was going on. And there were some thousand cruzeiro bills on the table. And a good steak on the kitchen counter.

—Did the old man invite you to eat?

He didn't have time, the neighbor with the broken bathtub straight from hell was waiting. But the little old man wrapped it up in some paper and gave it to him.

—He treated you like someone dying from hunger, like a beggar.

Fuck it! How can there be such careless people? they just leave their money lying around like that, but in forty minutes when he gets off this shitty bus his mother will cook him the steak. He'd share it with her—even half! But she can't eat meat because of her missing teeth.

—If you were a snake, who would you bite?

He's not in Cocotá right now, there aren't any snakes around here.

—Here's the situation, let's say you have to bite someone because you can't live with the poison, you have to choose a victim.

He has to choose a victim? It's all the same, a man or a woman?

—Who would you bite, a brother of yours or a sister?

He'd never do that. He'd bit that cow, he hated her so much he had to kill her, he turned her into shit with one shot.

—And that woman of your father's?

He doesn't hate her. As he grew up it all ended, yes? He wouldn't bite her, no way. Because the situation is as follows: When you're a kid you think one way, but later you find out what life is like, you become a man and that stuff, you think about it differently. Later on you understand that a married man never has only one woman, he generally has two, three, four, as many as possible, is that clear? When he was going with Gloria he had others. And all in all, he'd have to think about it, which of them he loved more. Gloria believed she was the main one, right? Let her believe it! If she's happier that way.

—That's not true! What I want to know is the truth about everything that happened.

And now that she's sick in the head she should keep on believing it.

—That's not true, I'm getting better and I want to know the truth and nothing else.

She can think whatever she wants, he's not going to die over it, why make a fuss, he's going to bed today with a full belly, what does he need her for? If she doesn't love him anymore he doesn't care. He had a woman who loved him a lot, because she knew very well that he was a straightforward man.

—How many thousand cruzeiros bills were on the old man's table this afternoon?

She lived in the country, on a farm, same as him.

—Don't tell me her name, please.

Azucena, with black hair, not blonde like María da Gloria.

— . . .

She took part in everything, the same as him, the things he liked, she was older than Gloria, on the soccer field she was also fanatic about the team, and her father hated him, he didn't want her to go to the field, but she was usually accompanied by a group of girlfriends, yes? So she went, no matter what.

— . . .

He told Gloria, "Azucena gives me what you never gave me, not because you don't have it, but because you never wanted to give it to me." He began making out with both of them, at the same time, he liked to make out secretly, well hidden, no one knew about it, a big secret. First he'd meet with one and then the other.

Azucena lived in the country so he had more opportunities to meet her during the day. While the other one lived in town. With the one from the country he'd make a date under the trees, is that clear? He'd say, "Hey so and so, I'll wait for you under such and such a tree at such and such an hour," and she'd wait, well hidden, no one would see her. But she was headstrong, that one, she truly loved him.

—But you didn't really love her, because she was from a farm.

So one time he went to play a game of soccer at a field very close to her father's farm, and back then there was another guy who liked her, and she knew it, the guy was a bullfighter. He fought in all the towns, he'd grab the bull by the head, all that, and her father wanted her to be this guy's girlfriend, while the boy from the farm never wanted to find himself face to face with Azucena's father. Until they met one day, he felt that tremendous rage, " Come here, boy, you're going after my daughter and I've already said I'm going to kill you, I'm going to cut off your balls with a scythe, because you're also going around with Rossi's daughter and you want to go out with my daughter too; shit, you have a load of women and that will not be, I'll kill her or I'll kill you, one of the two." He gave his daughter some crazy beatings, because of him. He really gave it to her. She said, "Fucking hell, my father hit me! I'm all bruised up because of you, don't you see? But I'll face anything, no matter what he does it's useless because he can't come between us." And that's how things went, the more the father hit her, the more she came looking for him, right? It was useless, because she went to his cousins' house, to his aunts' house to find him, she'd do anything to be with him, because when a woman has the hots for a guy she'll take on God and the devil to be with the guy. So far so good. So then one day she showed up, he still hadn't slipped it to her, and he told her not to go to the field the next day. She went. They got into a terrible fight during the game. Everyone against him.

—You were a farm boy who had nothing, why was everyone against you?

It started with his second goal. He made the first. By the third they were saying, this guy is a demon. The game didn't last the ninety minutes.

—Lies.

The fight started in the morning with someone from town who was envious because of soccer, they crossed paths, the one from the farm, and the other from the town who played ball very well, and the one from the farm opened his big mouth, "This afternoon—watch out! Because you have to guard me, I'm going to take two or three shots at you and I'm going to score a goal." So when he made the first goal nothing happened, but he made the second and the other one didn't even see the ball, and said: "I'm going to start kicking so you'll stop fucking around!" He kicked and kicked but couldn't reach him, the one from the farm fooled him again when he made his third goal, and it was right in the ribs, the one from town hit him with his fist in the ribs and so

when he hit him, "Are you looking for a fight, or what?"
Because the guy wasn't one of those guys who look for
fights. And the guy said, "You bet I'm looking for a
fight." And the one from the farm punched him a few
times and he started to use the guy as a club to hit the
others who were coming down on top of him, yes? It
was incredible, until he lifted the guy into the air and
threw him on top that heap of people who were coming
after him.

— . . .

The police were already on their way. So a guy, who
was the coach of the team, took him in his car, no one
else would touch him, he was completely drenched with
blood, other people's blood, he hadn't even gotten a
scratch. And that night there was a bullfight, that guy
was going to give it to the bull. So then he went home, but
before he went he said, "Hell, I have to talk to Azucena,
the hell with them! I have to talk to her." And he quickly
went over to where she was, "I'm at such and such a
place, I'll wait for you there." And she said, "It's impossible, I'm really sorry." She was crying, she couldn't
because the old man wouldn't let up a bit, he wouldn't
let her out for anything. He said, "Where will you be?"
She said, "I have to stay at the bullfight, I'm obligated
to." He went home, came back in his car, everyone else
had trucks. He went to the bullfight, saw her, her father.
She was sitting, her father on one side and on the other
side the guy, he can't remember his name now, dressed
up like a toreador with special clothes, what shit, right?
And that's his name, shit, shit was his first name and shit

was his last name. He doesn't know what came over him then, but in front of everyone in the world he went up to her and said, "How are you, my love?" and he gave that little hand a squeeze. Her father gave the daughter a slap in the face that turned her purple. Then he pulled her over to him, "You're not going to hit her again! I'd like to see if you have the guts to hit her again!" Shit whore, so the father and the guy threw themselves on top of him. It was unbelievable, the bullfight was finished. He grabbed her and told her to get into his car and he shut the door and went back to settle the score with the others. So the group he'd gotten ready got together and set the bull free, everyone in the world went running, he set the tent on fire. She didn't love the guy, the father forced her to go out with him, what shit, she had to decide one way or the other, but the other one had complete freedom in the old man's house and he didn't. The guys got out their knives and revolvers and everything was burning, then the girl got into the car and they left in a procession, honking their horns, beep-beep-beep, to scare the public—which was already running—even more. The grandstand was full and it was coming down and you could hear them in a hush, "That boy is unbelievable, hell, he fought with everyone in the world and he gave it to everyone in the world, he came to the bullfight, he beat the hell out of everyone and now he calmly leaves." They went far away, not to Cocotá because they didn't want to make trouble, then they got daring and went to eat popcorn near another town around there, "My love, the situation is as follows:

What more do you want? Are you ready to run away with me?" and she, "Yes, I'll go wherever you take me! I'm in your hands."

—Farm people are different from town people.

Country people are completely different, right? People from town know more, they even make fun of people from the country. Country people speak differently, they speak badly, when they're in front of someone they don't say the right thing. People from São Paulo don't either, it seems like they're always singing, they don't speak clear Portuguese. And people from town always dress well and country people are humble people, they're as happy with very good clothes as with ordinary clothes. They dress simply. They go barefoot a lot, so that's why people from town think they're peculiar, so they say, "That's a farmer, he's barefoot."

—And their hair? Is that different too?

When they're going down the country road and a bus goes by it raises the dust and their hair gets all dusty, right? And so the other people whisper to each other, "That's a farmer." And that kind of thing. They start shouting and making fun of the guy, it's true, to put the person down, they're always trying to put down people from the country. So much that when country people get to town they're already afraid, right? that someone will shout something, they're already distrustful when they get there, right?

—And how did I speak?

Wonderfully well, a very pretty voice, of a feminine woman, speaking perfectly correctly. You didn't insult

people from the country, you treated everyone the same.
He told her he was from town, because he was born in
the hospital in town, and then he was raised on the farm.
And that later he'd been all over, in the State of Rio, in
the State of São Paulo. He said to her, "How will you be
able to love me, knowing my father lives on a farm?"
And she, "The important thing is that you are you."
Back then she never fainted, her mother told him, she
took her to a number of doctors and stuff like that, a
nervous problem, this and that, nothing came of it, the
only thing that happened was that they stopped going
out and just stayed home. And what he figured out in his
mind was the following: She started making scenes so
that they'd tell him and he'd come back to Cocotá, she
did those things like in a show, so that he'd hear about it
and come and help her, right?

—Then it wasn't true that I was feeling bad? Do I lie,
too?

He should forget about his worries because he's traveling comfortably sitting on this bus and when he gets
home he'll have a good steak.

—What did I want you to do to get ahead in life?

After taking her away in the car from that place where
the bullfight was, the hard part was giving her back to
her father, Azucena. That was no joke. He stayed with
her, he took her to his house, but when they arrived his
mother wouldn't accept her. It was incredible. It was the
biggest mess he ever created in his life.

—There's a thousand cruzeiros too many in your
pocket that don't belong to you.

He still hadn't touched her. He left her normal. Then
t.̣ ⌐ father showed up and said that he'd kill her or he'd
kill him, that he'd take her back and hit her, so he took
her and gave her a hell of a thrashing. She quietly let him
hit her, she told her father it was useless, right? It didn't
matter how much he hit her, she wasn't going to cry. "It's
useless, I'm not going to cry." So the more he hit her the
less she was going to cry. After a long time she still had
marks from the whip. And some fifteen days passed
without them seeing one another. They wouldn't let her
out. After the fifteen days he said to himself, talking to
himself like a crazy person, "Shit on your soul, where is
that woman, could her father have killed her?" So he
did the following, he had a friend who lived very near
her house, so he went to his friend's house to see if he
could see her from afar. And the friend said to him, hell,
he knew all about it, "Shit on that mother-fucking asshole
of an old man, the poor thing is suffering horribly because of you! Every day the bastard gives her an awful
beating!" Then he himself said, "Son of a bitch, I have
to do something about it!" So she had a sister who also
liked him, in two ways, to make out secretly with and
sometimes she also passed him notes from the sister,
that was the thing. And that sister saw him at the neighbor's house, sucking on a stalk of cane and she said
hello to him. So he asked her how she was and that kind
of thing. So she started showing him the place where
the old man let her have it with the whip, but she wasn't
Azucena whose body was all purple, but the sister, and
she showed him her back and all of her legs, very close

to the ass, "He hit her here, here, and here." He felt very badly about Azucena, he has a big heart.

—The old man gave you the steak, he had no idea what was going on.

Then he said to the friend, "Let's go over there." So the father wasn't home, "What are you doing?" And she, "Every day Papa hits me, a lot, and at night he brings over that Mancarrón guy, that's the toreador, they call him by his nickname, Old Horse. He brings him over every day and I have to sit next to him. I'm dying of rage." And that afternoon she left home and he brought her to live at this old lady's house, she was the best woman the fucking world has ever known in it's fucking life. She had one of the nicest homes in the countryside. And the old lady made the business ninety percent easier. She told him, "I'll take her into my home, but you can't be hanging around here, my boy; you can take her out, I'll take her in as a daughter but I won't give you the opportunity to do what you shouldn't." The old lady had another one like Azucena who also lived in the house because she was an unwed mother, but her name was Teresa and she was black.

—The old lady took her in as a servant, Teresa was the old lady's servant, too. The old lady was Olga's grandmother. There was another servant at Olga's house.

But he doesn't remember. That old lady had had children, but they were all married by then and she was alone with the old man, she wanted company. He brought his brother who was raised with him who was also black, for Teresa. So he and the black from hell, making their game plan, "Hell, we're really going to slip it to them!" He himself set up a perfect plan. He was the one who always set everything up, "Today we're going to carry out the following plan." And they were looking at the mango field, some unbelievable mango trees, sucking on mangoes and all that, with the two of them, watching the stream, making out, attacking them hard with their fingers. He put it to her this way, "Tonight I'm sleeping in your bed." And she, "But how will you do it? The old lady will know and she'll throw me out." Because Azucena had begun to respect the old lady the way she should. So he told her, "It's useless because after all this, after you've already had so many beatings because of me, and I have too, now we have to have our return match."

—Azucena was an Indian.

He was afraid one day her father would show up on the riverbank, with the Old Horse. They'd lie in wait for him. But he never saw him again at night, only during the day, in town. And the old lady handed her over on a silver platter, without realizing. And the four of them were making out in the sugarcane field, but making out hard, a matter of heavy artillery, and he told her, "Later we'll come up, me and the black one, to sleep with the two of you," one on one side and the other on the other side, because the bed was very big. The four of them started to inspect the house, it was two stories, "We have to do the following: put up a ladder, look for that ladder early and put it up, pretending you're grabbing oranges from the tree high up on the ladder." So she did, she leaned the ladder against an orange tree, then against another one, meanwhile it was starting to get dark, when it got very dark he told her to put the ladder right beneath the window. She placed it to the millimeter. So he could climb up and jump inside. Dinnertime came, Azucena and Teresa went to take a bath, too. So when it was ten o'clock, more or less, they showed up. So it was time for the old lady's old husband to get back from town, to his big house. They were climbing the ladder when they heard the old man on the horse, clop-clop-clop, and they jumped down again, hidden behind some plants. "We'll wait awhile." But they couldn't stand it anymore, minutes passed, "Fucking hell, I can't stand it anymore." And she was nervous waiting with the window open. But the old man came in with his boots and the floor of the house was tile and he made a hell of a racket. So the window was open, they jumped in, they stayed until five in the morning. He with one, the black one with the other, they had goose bumps they were so horny.

— . . .

Son of a bitch, what a mess that was, but she couldn't take it and he held back like a beginner instead of attacking and that's that, he did it slowly and that kind of thing, a lot worse, playing around, but he drove her wild, and that way the whole night passed.

— . . .

He put it between her legs at the little mouth that was closed, and he pushed. So each day she got a big poke, right? So she's saying, yes, no, until one day he grabbed it impatiently, he forced it with all his life and soul and it exploded all over the place. And immediately he went back to his house. And the whole world was at peace.

— . . .

Women have a lot of tricks, it's better not to pay too much attention to them, just stick it in.

—I don't know when to believe you and when not to.

He did go into her, and from then on it went in completely fine. That day when he was going to open her she said like this, "Oooh, I have to stand it!" And she ordered him to just go ahead with everything he had. Every day he'd force it a little, but that day he got through to the other side, and he felt it going through and she shrieked. She said, "Son of a bitch, it's there." So he hurt himself too that day, he gave it a period of four or five days to recover, after that he kept it up, bang-bang-bang, but she was tight as can be, unbelievable. He did it to her every which way, on her back, on her stomach, he'd mount her in every position. She didn't complain, ever, she liked it any way they did it, on the edge of the bed, on the floor, standing up, the thing was for him to keep banging. Every afternoon he'd go to train at the soccer field in town, after that he'd take a bath, he'd have dinner at Olga's house, then cross the street, and make out with María da Gloria as long as he pleased.

—Why did they feed you for free at Olga's house? I want to know the truth.

He was a good son. Every night he accompanied his mother back to the farm. Everyone said the same thing, "Josemar is a very good son." Olga's mother, Olga, everyone. And after that he'd go through the cane fields again, the mango trees, and he met Azucena on the road, the ladder wasn't up. She knew he'd met María da Gloria in town, back then he didn't mount María da Gloria, he mounted her. But he'd get there all worked up from a lot of things and Azucena began to catch on, "Hell, you get here in a bad mood and you unload on me." And he, "Sure I unload on you," because he filled her cup full, "don't make trouble, I know which one of you is having a better time, because the other one isn't taking part in this festival like the young lady here; the other one hasn't even met this love stick, it's all yours." So she calmed down and accepted it all, but she just couldn't swallow the idea that he went out with the other one, the idea was for her to be the only one; and the other one, too, her idea was to be the only one. If there was a dance on the farms he'd tell Azucena, "Listen: you'll wait for me at such and such a dance, first I'm going to town, later I'll come back to the dance on the farms." "No, Josemar, you're coming straight to the dance." And he'd just turn his back to her and leave without saying a thing. And she, "I'll wait for you at the dance, my love." Because she knew that later she would be the winner.

—I'm going to get better soon so I can go to dances again.

No, he doesn't believe it, and he told María da Gloria

on that occassion that he was a man and he had to keep
telling Azucena lies, telling her he loved her. He invited
María da Gloria to go for a walk in the countryside, at
night, without her parents knowing. She said she didn't
like that because at night in the country you couldn't see
the birds or the flowers that grow by themselves without
anyone planting them. Then he told her that those things
couldn't be seen at night but to look at the moon and the
clouds which were very pretty, and the stars. "You have
to learn and remember to go out to look at them, and
that way your sadness will pass."

—I'm never sad, my mama's very good, my papa's
very good, my house is one of the prettiest in town.

And he said, "But I'm sad; if you don't give me what
I ask for I'll go spend the night in that old lady's house
who's so good and lets me come and stay with Azucena;
and I'll climb up the ladder and if Azucena has a child
of mine I'll have to marry her." He kept saying that if
he married Azucena he'd bring her to live on his farm,
his mother lives in one house and she has another one
in back, right? It's a shed, just one room, very modest,
with that roof of all different tiles, from the old days,
right? And between them a lot of banana trees and an
orange plant that grew, and now it's higher than everything and it's giving oranges. He told María da Gloria
that if she didn't give it to him he'd have to keep on
seeing Azucena. Gloria had turned fourteen and they
watched her very carefully at night, "Tomorrow, Sunday,
in the afternoon I'll tell my mother that I'm going to study

with my girlfriend who lives the farthest away and I'll
go to your farm." And he told her not on a Sunday because his mother was there at the farm all day.

—It has to be tomorrow, Sunday, because I can't stand
it anymore.

He met her halfway there, where no one couldn't see
them, they went into the thicket and into the farm by
the back way. He'd prepared a clean bed, all white. She
was trembling because it would be the first time. He
opened her dress and began to suck on her breasts, which
were already bursting. She said it was too bad it wasn't
night so that they could look at the clouds and the moon,
which were pretty, and the stars, that way your sadness
passes. He said he wasn't sad because it was the hap-
piest day of his life, the day of his wedding. And then
she said they shouldn't lose any more time, she wanted
to be his wife, that way they'd never again be separated.
And he said he was going to open her up completely,
now, that way her father couldn't throw him into the
street for being poor and uneducated. Yes, because their
enemy was her father, her mother liked him.

—But who's there? Who opened the door? Who came
in like a fury, screaming at you? Who took you out and
is slapping you so hard? Who's ruining your life forever?

The orange tree hadn't grown yet and you could see
the shed out back, from the kitchen of the farm. The
mother saw that someone had gone in, some thieves, she
thought and she came out with a broom to scare them
away, "What kind of mess are you getting into here?

And with other peoples' daughter! Oh, you punk you'd better watch your step!" And all those things people say. And he said, "No, ma'am, don't hit me like that, I didn't even get far enough to undress her completely! Don't you see there wasn't enough time for anything to happen?" Because with his mother there was a very serious problem, right? She wanted everything to be correct, right? And he realized that . . . what was it he realized? That the old lady was capable of telling María da Gloria's mother. If he brought her back to the shed again.

—When you get back to your house don't tell your mother that she did something bad to you, she's very sick now. But she did you a wrong that will never be set right.

It's been a long time since he's heard anything about Gloria, all he asks is that God protect her. Or if she gets better that she doesn't forget him.

—Your mother is sick, too, don't reproach her for anything, what good would it do? When you get back give her the steak and she'll cook it for you with a little rice.

Chapter Six

—Why is the house so dirty? No one washed last night's dinner dishes. Today when you came in tired from working all day you saw an unmade bed.

He got back from work at nine o'clock at night, fucking Rio, so far from his house, he slept on the bus the whole way. Because, hell, there's nothing new to see. One of these days they're going to steal his wallet and he'll be left without papers, the old lady already left him without any money. She went to the farm, she's sick, a sixteen hour train ride is cheaper, but she got there alive, he asked God to let her be able to stand the trip and if she didn't get there alive someone would have sent him a telegram. The oldest daughter will take care of her on the farm until she's better, is that clear? That way she's spared the operation. He still hasn't recovered totally from her last operation, he already had a lot of financial setbacks, he's been left without liquid assets, yes? He never went up to her and said, "Mama, I haven't got a cent." Because of the following: because she's very good and could say, "My son, you could have let me die, that way you wouldn't be left without any money, right?" He had nothing left but what he'd scraped together to buy himself a car, he was finally going to have a car in his life, "My son, do you have any money left, so you can live without trouble?" And he, "Sure I have." What he has left now is the roof over his head and that's it, in the little house in Santísimo.

—What's Santísimo like? I've never been there, the name is pretty, a saint who protects you from all dangers. But he doesn't protect you at all.

There are hills, a jungle, on the outskirts, and in Santísimo there are supermarkets, shops are making a lot of progress, they grow from one day to the next. And a pretty bus terminal, all modern, right? where every bus leaves for other states, other, totally different places. All electronic, right? It functions all automatically. And the other buildings aren't old, none of that. New and they're getting newer, because they're demolishing the ones that were the old, and now the new television antennas on a hill. Pretty houses with tile roofs and a few of them they're never going to tear down, he passed by one that said 1910 on the front, and that one they're never going to get rid of because it's old, very strong construction, is that clear? Because back then cement didn't cost anything, they took it from there in the rocks in the mountains, which nowadays costs 1,500 cruzeiros a bag. And in the area where the houses end, there are other more modest ones, and years ago his father left the countryside because the farm wasn't producing anything then, to work as a stevedore in the harbor. He bought a piece of land in installments and with the son he built a house with only one room, and the kitchen, and then the bathroom, and then another room. But the father wanted to go back to the countryside and he and the mother stayed on for good. Why doesn't the saint protect him?

—If it rains at night there's a roof to keep the rain out.

All he has left is that roof, but if the mother has to go back for an operation the only thing he'll have to sell is that little house. If she needs the money he won't be able to tell her not to sell it, right?

—Why don't you like them to spy on you from the house across the street? Why do they give you dinner there every night at Olga's house? Why do they let you in if when you turn your back they call you the farm boy?

Today, Friday, at night there should be a dance on the farms, he made it there late from Gloria's house, he'd gone to the house of a friend of hers and back to Gloria's house, where he had plenty of freedom, he was very well respected in that establishment, on that property, as they say. So usually he was stuck there until late, and one night when he was able to get away he went to the dance on the farms with Rogerio, he re-

members as if it were yesterday, a friend who also had a
girlfriend very near Gloria's house, so they both agreed
on the exact hour they'd go to the dance, so then the
other one showed up first, punctual, and waited for him,
the two of them on bicycles, but in the dark because they
didn't have lanterns. So when they were halfway there,
he was dressed all in white giving it all he had on the
bicycle, he was ahead, there was an ox in the middle of
the road, "God free me and save me!" But he couldn't
brake in time and he ran over the bull and went right
over him, and the other guy also goes and smashes into
the bull and breaks the handlebar of the bicycle. Hell,
it was incredible, they left the bike hidden there in the
thickets. Rogerio climbed onto the bar of the bike and
they continued on their way to the dance, but they
arrived all dirty, with a wounded forehead and scratches
all over, the elbows, the arms, right? Incredible, but just
ahead the dance was good, accordion music and a lot to
stuff your face with. A little while later Rogerio un-
covered the snake pit and died. But so that night the girls
were all worried, the other guy also had a spare girlfriend from the farms. So he showed up like that in that
darkness at the edge of the dance floor, he looked and
saw Azucena leaning against a jaca plant, pretty sad. So
he arrived like that, he grabbed her from behind and
gave her a big kiss, as if a bomb had exploded, smack!
and she said, "But my God, you sure are late enough!
They've already served a keg of beer, they served the
cake already, I don't know what else, grilled meat." So
he said, "It's not important, I know what concerns me

and it's well guarded." And upon saying that he gave her a slap on the fattest part of her ass, yes? And she was still mad, and he said to her, "You didn't save me any of that beer they passed around, right? And you didn't save me any cake, either, so you'll have to give me something. And that's what I came looking for, not the fucking beer or the fucking cake, understand?" So she said, "Hell, this guy's got some nerve!" She complained, she talked a bit too much, but later on everything straightened itself out, they went to dance, is that clear? Samba, bolero, waltz. She had a lot of favorite songs but he doesn't remember their names, he doesn't remember the name of any song. Azucena also liked Roberto Carlos, when he started out as a singer. He remembers one of those pieces, the one that said that the leaves fall but they grow back again. Gloria also liked that one, both of them liked Roberto Carlos, they really adored him. He came twice to sing at the dance in town, and it was the end of the world, both chicks went to hear him, so he couldn't manage it so one of them would pay attention to him, he went and gave one a kiss and then gave the other a kiss, he was running around the dance all night long until finally what always happened happened. He left Gloria first, he took her home and went back to the farms with Azucena. He walked with her, on the usual road where he left the bicycle that time the boy also slammed into the ox, Rogerio, who died later.

—Do you always remember Rogerio?

No, it's been a long time since he's thought of Rogerio. People forget when someone dies, no one remembers anymore. It was him, the one with Azucena on the road to the farms, it wasn't Rogerio who went with Azucena, even though he was still alive back then, it was him, Josemar, doesn't everyone remember him? He's alive right now, Josemar, everyone remembers him, right? They were on the road, they stopped to rest, what's called the good life, if he wasn't with one chick he was with the other, he had others, too, women always sprung up around him, so that thing was as follows: it seemed that he was the sheriff, out in the Far West with lots of gold in the bank in town, but it wasn't because of that, it was that he had women falling all over him. All those guys really were loaded with gold, with really big cars, but they didn't get what he got. Those papa's boys, right? Sons of millionaires, all of them asked him, "Hey, Josemar! How do you get so many women? We're not getting anything." He said, "Go to Hell, don't ask me, I don't know how it's done, and why make a fuss, it's my problem, you want me to give you lessons?" And so what he did was laugh at them while he promised to open their eyes. But they were no good for that, right?

— . . .

For him those were good times, what he needs to do now is to resolve his problems, he wants to resolve all his problems this year, to live life a little more, because lately he hasn't lived at all. Hell, the problem with work on the one hand and on top of that his mother's illness, he's really screwed. So he doesn't have time, he doesn't have the means, he doesn't get the time to forget himself and dedicate a little time to sex, is that clear? For a guy to enjoy the sexual side he has to forget about everything, yes? He should be able to say, I'm not owing money to anyone nor having problems with anyone. That's the way it should be, that way they could go fuck themselves if he didn't work one day, or two, everything in order. He shouldn't go on pulling out his hair. Yes? It's that he doesn't like being alone in the house without the old lady.

— . . .

There are times when Gloria doesn't think about him. Long stretches of time. It must be when she's asleep. He hopes she rests, with a very peaceful sleep. But when she wakes up she'll remember, right? Because she was healthy, strong, right? One hell of a blonde. She had no reason to get sick and have bad nerves. Her family wasn't like that. That last summer it was boiling hot, and he spent it with María da Gloria beneath the mango tree. She was wearing shorts, very short, with half her cheeks showing, he'd go half silly, he couldn't look at it, it drove him crazy, is that clear? Then they rested against the tree, hours chatting, they climbed up the branches, she climbed up too, she climbed until she was above everything, to grab the mangoes, he stayed below and looked at those cheeks, that whole game. And he had a few more women who gave it to him. Gloria didn't, now they were in the final stages, he was getting everything ready to leave town, he remembers those times they went out, she was already different, she'd begun to panic, she was really losing control, she wasn't the same girl as before, she was waiting for some change in things, realizing that something could happen. So since that moment he felt that something bad could happen. So he moved away very suddenly, like those drops of water striking the coals of fire. And what he did was to cook her over a slow fire, he steamed her, preparing her well, to leave her.

— . . .

How was it that he prepared her? It was as follows: back then they met every day, that was a firm date. Normally from eight at night until eleven, twelve at night, then he began to go twice a week and he wouldn't stay as long on the weekend, the hours they spent together were getting fewer. He'd say to her like this, "Tomorrow I'll be here at such and such an hour." And he wouldn't show up at that hour, he'd get there like one hour, or two or three hours later. And he'd leave earlier than he used to. It was almost time to leave town and she had to give it to him before he left.

— . . .

She'd say, "You didn't come last night and this morning I took it out on my plants, I didn't water them at all because of you; the garden will get ugly, you'll see." And down there they have a rice fiesta, at the beginning of winter, thousands of people gather there, right? In that town. So on that date the three would be at the same old place, Gloria, Azucena, and a teacher who was also giving it to him. And Gloria's friend, who doesn't count, four women on the lookout for him, in that little town. So he had to disappear, sometimes he went to the bar, where they had billiards. Hours and hours playing billiards while she was going after him, going here, going there, searching for him. That's why he called a friend, "I challenge you to a game of billiards, let's play, because I have such and such a problem." So that's where he'd go and he'd stay there and play for hours, toc-toc-toc. It turned eight at night, nine, ten, the rice fiesta went on, Gloria, since she was very bright, went looking for him from bar to bar, where could he have gone? Because whenever she asked he'd say, "I was playing billiards." And things along that line. So she found him at ten-thirty, more or less. She saw him, she sent someone to call him inside the bar there. So he sent someone to say, "No way, because I'm playing a game with a money bet and all that, I can't attend to you now, understand? You'd better entertain yourself with your mother." She says, but this but that, she wouldn't give up, she came back again a few more times, he didn't show up, "Oh, you're hiding because of all the women going by here. I know there's a bunch of shameless bitches going around saying I don't know what, that I'm your girlfriend and they're going to hit me, all that kind of thing." So he said, "They're not going to hit you at all, nothing of the kind, don't be silly, understand? You're all friends with one another." So he finished with his little game and left with her. But the problem for her was whether to stay in the street where the others could see her with him, is that clear? So he said to himself, "Fucking son of a bitch, this won't work because the others are going to take it badly and I'll lose all those females, will I wind up with only one?" So he struggled with her to take her straight home. He said, "Oh, I'm not feeling well, my love, I have to go, let's go right to your house, OK?" She said, "OK." But then she wouldn't budge from the door of the bar. So he grabbed her arm and said, "Let's go, once and for all." So they went to her house, they got there, she was all serious, she said he was hiding her. So generally the mother used to go into the living room, that night she said, "You're talking a lot today." Because generally those two didn't do much talking, right? It was a matter of a lot of bartering of kisses, caresses, one passing a hand smoothly over the other's, they'd hardly say a word, it was more a matter of putting the hand here or putting it there, and giving those special hugs, all that kind of thing, is that clear? That's when they started with those trunks of tongues down the throat, which were just unbelievable. When a little female kisses well, with those little licks, a guy can go half crazy, or totally crazy.

— . . .

Where on earth did Azucena end up? He'd wish her well, single or married, whatever, but very happy, like she was before, with him. Before he left town, before so much time passed, before his mother got sick, and these greasy plates were stacked up in the kitchen sink. And before he threw those sons into the world that María da Gloria never saw.

—Where are your children?

She believed it, one of his lies, a joke he thought about pulling on her one day, to see if she'd believe him, but it could also be to help her get over her sickness, one day

Gloria would see a little boy of four pass by, or of six, both looking exactly like him, and that could help her wait a little longer until she could see him in the flesh.

—Is that true?

One is four, the most rebellious, the other is six.

—Who's the mother?

He didn't have a son, a woman had his son. He really loves his son, is that clear? In Santísimo. As a matter of fact, there are two altogether, not just one son. One with one woman and another with a different one.

—Do they look like you?

They're not to be believed, distrustful, rebellious, but he doesn't live with them, right? He lives completely apart, no ties, but they walk by together occasionally, no problem. They look alike. From different mothers but they took after him. He loves them a lot, with all his soul, he feels bad he can't give them all the support he'd like. That's why he goes around always saying that life is more complicated than hell.

—Do they love you?

They call him papa. No, now they're with some other man, with a stepfather. It's as follows: the woman who has anything to do with him always ends up loving him a lot, and she's left in this state of expectation. Waiting for him to return. But he'll never return. He'll show up and disappear again.

—These women keep waiting for you?

He thinks the following: His sons, he'd like them to be soccer players, right? He'd do everything possible to teach the sons to be soccer players, that's where the money is; or if not, to study and stuff like that. But who's going to put up with paying for their education until they grow up? Which is fucking expensive, isn't it? So, let's say, if he could now he'd pay for a private school, but he can't, how could he? His pockets are the way they are, he doesn't even have enough to buy them clothes. When the right moment comes he's going to pay for private school for the smaller one. It's that he loves them a hell of a lot. He hasn't taken his eyes off them from the time they were born to this day. A father generally wants all the best for a son, for him to be a well-educated son, well prepared, an affectionate kid, is that clear? And that's the way they are. They no sooner set eyes on him than they're running up to him and grabbing him, kissing him, when they go by with the mother from afar, "Oh, there's my father!" And that kind of thing, "I'm going to give him a kiss!" And they come running, they hug him, they kiss him, then they're on their way, they're off, no problem. To their neighborhood, far away from his house because Santísimo is a small town but not so small. But sometimes they turn up there, too, at his house, no problem. She drops in once in a while, too, they haven't come to blows, right? They exchange ideas, they have a little chat now and then. The only thing is they don't have relations anymore now.

—Weren't there two women?

He never lived with her. He'd go to see her, they'd go around together. She's a teacher at the city school, she used to have a car, she'd go by and call him to go out, so OK, he'd let her invite him, "You can take me wherever you want, no problem." She'd invite him to go out, to go to the beach, he'd eat shrimp and she'd sunbathe, then they'd leave and he'd mount her in the car, the thing was to have a good time, and what's wrong with that?

— . . .

The other one too. The same thing, the two were the same, they were friends with one another. One introduced the other one. The friend enjoyed him so he had both of them at the same time. He'd go out with one of them, he'd go out with the other, because neither of them knew it, that he was going out with the other one. Two teachers. So they kept going out and they ended up with bellies. They knew how to take care of themselves, no problem, they left it like that. Two kids were born. Sometimes he carries the picture in his wallet. Two males, males like the father. He has a picture of their birthday party, he always participates on that day. A little while ago it was his birthday. A bad year, he didn't get anything, hell, he's still waiting, something can still turn up from somewhere. What he wouldn't like is if they got married, twenty years from now who knows what could happen in the world, better for them to be alone without problems.

— . . .

He knew the thing to do was wait, one day María da Gloria would give it to him. He started to grope her, after fifteen days of making out, "And when are you going to serve me that dish?" So she didn't understand,

"I have the body of a young lady, but I haven't turned thirteen yet." But he began breaking down her restraint.

— . . .

They'd been going together over a year, that day she started to cry. He said, "I'm leaving you because there's no reason not to give me complete freedom. Like to run my hand over your beautiful body." So she was looking at him and he said, "Quick, don't miss that chameleon, look at it go up that wall! What a pretty chameleon!" So she turned around to look and he grabbed her from behind and put his hand right on top of that fat mouth between her legs. She was really startled, "What's this?! You can't do . . ." And then he began kissing, biting, sucking, and with his finger always working on that little nest. And that's how he was, creak, creak, creak, he kept tightening the screws one by one. And so when four or five months had passed, with him always fingering her, smoothing that hairdo down there, one day he grabbed her hand and put it on top of him. She left it there a moment and then she quickly took it off. And time was passing, generally when he had his finger there, right? Then he'd grab her hand and put it where it should go, to get her used to it. Until one day she put her hand there and didn't take it off.

—I put my hand there myself?

No, he took her hand and made her put it there and said, "Right there, don't take that pretty hand away until it learns how to grab." To the point where she began to get used to it, every day she left it longer. One day she stroked it for ten minutes, or fifteen, and later on she caressed it one hour, two, three, four, right? And that way she started going crazy with excitement, every time they met he gave her the same proof of affection, and she him, until he made her feel really good, she covered his finger with honey. And at times he had to be careful because she'd scratch him with her fingernails from so much excitement. And that was just with his finger, nothing else, and a finger isn't the same as that other thing, a finger feels good, but that thing fills and expands. And time passed that way, until she liked it too much. So he said to her, "Now there's only one thing missing." She said she didn't know how that thing was done. And he told her she could put herself on top or on the bottom, any way she liked, without the slightest problem. And she, "But it's going to hurt a lot." And he, "Hell, what's going to hurt! Everyone does it and it doesn't hurt anyone." And she, "Heck, it's not that easy." And he, "Agreed, one of these days you're going to accept it." And she kept making progress and one day he told her, "It's agreed that we're going to do it on such a day at such and such an hour, and the subject is closed." But the time came and she wouldn't let him. She said no. So he disappeared from her house for three days, four, a week. And she was left to think, she'd go crazy when she didn't see him, she'd go out and he'd hide from her, that kind of thing. Until he returned, he let from one Sunday to the next go by without seeing her. So when Sunday came around he showed up at her house around eight at night. So in the end there wasn't any trouble, she came over, "Hey, you disappeared!" And who knows what else, she kissed him, all that, "Why did you go so many days without seeing me, didn't you miss me?" And he, "Sure I missed you, but as it happened you wouldn't play my game that day and that kind of thing, you didn't accept my proposition." So he let several days go by, like a month, hands still, serious, not saying anything more about it. But after that he changed again, he started teasing her again, bringing up the same conversation, "When is it going to be? I'm waiting." She was dodging him, she was trying to dodge him. "You're playing with me, you're giving me a hard time, you don't really like me at all," and stuff like that. "But don't get upset because one day we're going to do it, what I need is a guarantee, will we get married afterward?" And he, "Sure we'll get married, I want to get married, I really love you." And she, "But then to do that we'll have to get married before we thought we would." That's when he took advantage to fill her with hopes, right? "Of course we'll get married, urgently, maybe this will be a step so that our marriage can happen more quickly," he told her, and she said, "That's not possible." So then they set a date and she showed up. It was in the country, out there in a special place there were some trees—but no, not here thrown on the ground like that, it wasn't possible, not a little girl with class, not the kind to throw herself on the ground, so hell! Without a cent, on the sly, he couldn't take her to a hotel or anything, so they went back to town, he thought about that shed of the mother's, that shed out back, and secretly from the mother he started getting everything ready for the day. He told Gloria, "There's a shed behind my house and no one will see us there." He started to arrange everything at night, they spent some time making plans, he got a mattress, an old mattress, he told her, "Mama, you have to throw out this shitty old mattress!" And she, "That's true, then we'll see about buying a new one, so we can get rid of this one." And he, "Throw this mattress out, it's useless, it's all old and full of holes." And she, "Where will you throw it, son? Behind the old house?" Because that's what she called the shed, "You can leave it right there, I'll take care of it, I'll put it behind the shed, you know?" And so later, when she wasn't paying attention, around seven at night, he went into the shed and set up a perfect bed, he'd already stolen a bedspread from the sister, he went to his sister's house and took a bedspread, "But what are you doing?" And he, "Nothing, it's to cover my face with so no one knows who I am, to scare a guy who played a dirty trick on me." And the sister, "Watch out, that guy might be armed and shoot you if he doesn't recognize you." "Nothing like that, why would he shoot me? it's all a joke." So she handed him the bedspread, "It's pretty old, I don't need it anymore." So then he went all the way over there to find Gloria and they went for a walk, looking at the moon and the stars, now he wasn't the only one who liked them because she did too, and when they were almost there she wanted to turn back, and he, "Hell, if you leave I'll kill you!" Angry as a son of a bitch. But he'd already told her mother they'd be back a little late because they were going with some girlfriends to such and such a place,

"All right, my daughter is yours, but she's not yours that much yet, I'll let you go out for a little while and that kind of thing, but not so you can do whatever you want, she's still not really yours." But she always said that kidding around, the mother. So finally they left. Gloria had never been there, she hadn't seen the house and they went in by the back door of the shed, you can see the other door from the kitchen window, and the brothers already knew all about it, right? Those guys talked to each other, "Let's go over and listen to everything." The sons of bitches came over and stayed there listening, he'd told them that day there'd be a hell of a racket, because it was the first time anyone had mounted Gloria, but he quickly shut the door tight, and the windows. They didn't hear a thing, the assholes. He broke down her restraint immediately, that way she didn't have time to repent, what she started to feel was very cold, like Azucena the first time. She cried from pain and started to tremble, she got goose bumps and when the cold began to get worse and make her tremble and turn pale it was because he was coming to the final blow, like with Azucena, she yelled, she made a tremendous racket, she cried, "Oh, oh my God! Oh, how I adore you!" And the pain, it was killing her, she said.

—You told me the first time was in a hotel, why so many lies? Or was it lying in the grass, right there in the countryside, the first time?

No, in a hotel people saw her go in. No, nothing like that. But it hurt so badly she wanted to die, even though between the pain and the pleasure, which of the two did she choose? It was an unbelievable thing, between the pain and the pleasure she decided to keep feeling the pleasure.

—No matter how hard I try I can't remember that pain. Really, I can't.

Poor Gloria, she isn't well in the head. It's that she imagines things, she gets attacks, she feel bad and she screams, but not like that day, that day she screamed because he hurt her, he hurt bad enough to kill her.

—After you left town I wanted to feel that pain again, so I could remember what it was like—or is it that I never felt it?

Her mother told him that one day Gloria scratched her breast with her nails, right over her heart, to feel pain, until she drew blood. But then the mother went running, she grabbed a pair of scissors and cut her nails. She'd never scratched herself before because at first when she began to miss him so much she scratched the wall with her nails, thinking it was him.

Chapter Seven

—I want you to swear to tell me the truth.

He's going to tell Gloria the whole truth about what happened before and after her sickness.

—Swear on your mother's life.

It'll do Gloria good to know the whole truth, if he tells her all of it nicely it's sure to make her feel better. He swears to tell her the whole truth, he swears it on the life of his sainted mother, today, Saturday afternoon, with a pile of cruzeiros in his pocket, enough for Monday's bus fare and a pack of cigarettes, and besides he has a lot in his bank account, his honor and that's it. Hell. This morning the mother of his two sons told him he wasn't a man of his word, that bitch! That's what she said, that he'd never confronted the truth of things in his life, "Josemar, sometimes the truth hurts but you have to face it, if not what kind of man are you? A chickenshit! What kind of man is afraid of the truth? It takes more than a pair of balls to make a real man." She was blind with rage because he ran into her in the street and he couldn't give her even one cent.

—But you will tell me the truth. I believe you.

On his mother's life, he swears. He's a man and he's not afraid of anything, if he made a mistake at a certain point in his life, he asks forgiveness, and next time everything will turn out completely fine, won't it?

—I'm listening.

According to María da Gloria's mother she kept seeing him, even though he was far away, yes? "My daughter tells me she sees you coming with a bouquet of flowers, bigger every time, so big it won't fit in her arms."

—No, what happened to me doesn't matter, I want to know about you.

It's that it all began that Monday morning, when he left town and he didn't want to sleep during the trip so he could see all the new sights, but later he couldn't remember everything he'd seen, he was thinking a lot about the whole business, no? About the night before, everything he'd talked about with Gloria, and he didn't see all the sights and stuff like that, on the road. He had to change buses to get to Baurú, there were three buses standing there, one to Baurú, he doesn't remember where the other one went, and the other one was going back the way he'd come, he'd take that one and in the morning he'd be back in Cocotá, and he'd walk less than an hour and he'd be on

the farm, he could have hugged the mother before she left
the house like every morning. He didn't have enough for
the fare, that's why he didn't go back. In Baurú the ones
who finished electrician's studies went into the electric
company when there was work. But there was always
work. And from the company they sent him to the Grand
Baurú Boardinghouse. "Two more will be sleeping in the
room," the personnel office told him; on the farm he slept
with another brother across the bed with his feet under
his nose, until he grew up and then the little black slept
there, he was black but he didn't grow very tall and he
didn't reach any higher than his armpit. He didn't want
to sleep in the same bed with someone he didn't know, if
the guy was tall as hell what the new one could do was
sleep on the floor if he had something to cover himself
with, yes? But there were three beds in that room, one for
each of them. Two guys who had family right nearby,
they couldn't walk there, but on Friday night each one
went on his bike. His bed also had two sheets, like the
other guys'. María da Gloria, it seems she could see him
and talk to him, but every night that week the three of
them came back there to sleep and she, if she'd been there
in person in front of the other two she wouldn't have told
him anything, or asked him any questions, would she? On
Friday night he had to sleep alone and he'd never slept
by himself in one room. First he went to dinner, in the
boardinghouse they gave him coffee with milk and bread
in the morning, and a very delicious lunch, hell, and
dinner was very good, too, but that night he wasn't hungry. Her mother told him later that the worst for María

da Gloria, when her nerves got worst, was Sunday night,
Friday night she was happy because she started getting
ready for his visit, and since he didn't come she'd wait
until Saturday, and since he didn't come she'd wait until
Sunday night and that's when she'd start to cry, and that
stuff. And sometimes without any crying or hitting things
or anything, suddenly she'd faint. But for him Friday
night was the worst, if María da Gloria had known that
the other two had left the room, she, if she had been
in Baurú, would have been able to come in and tell
him whatever she wanted to, no one at all would have
heard her, but he kept quiet and heard the jukebox
in the boardinghouse, nothing else, whenever someone
threw in a chip. If he were in Cocotá he would have
wanted to ask her where she felt that pain, that made her
faint. The pain came from within, she would have said,
because she felt the same as he did, he didn't understand
these things, women do, when a person misses someone a
lot the pain is in the heart, "It's the same with me," he
would have told her, that pain that cuts from the inside
out. When people stopped putting change in the boardinghouse jukebox you could barely hear the people playing cards far away down in the bar, and then nothing
else, not a fucking thing. He'd go to bed and start to
think, yes? And the minute he'd take off his clothes to go
to sleep, he was putting everything over a chair and he'd
say, "Dog's luck, these clothes are completely different
from the kind she liked, what she always wanted me to
wear!" She had asked him to always wear something
black. They got along well in everything, they even liked

the same things, suits, clothes, yes? She liked the color black a lot, black clothes.

—That's true.

So then he'd always try to find out why she liked black clothes. But she didn't want to tell him. He would be alone in the silence of the room Friday night, Saturday morning, in the afternoon, at night, all day Sunday, if he wanted to he could have asked her any one of those things he didn't remember anymore, about the memories they both had, because the other two electricians couldn't hear him, but he couldn't see her because she was far away. He did have her picture and he looked at it often. And then he'd close his eyes to see if he could remember her face if he wasn't looking at the picture. At work way up on a high-voltage pole, waiting over an hour one time for replacements for some big screws, he wanted to remember her face and he couldn't remember either her face or her mother's face. Because María da Gloria looks like her mother, who's also tall, blond, with blue eyes, she's not skinny, and what else? More or less medium body, and the legs? Very pretty, no bruises, no cuts. Her body is totally unbelievable, it looks like a mold, doesn't it? He didn't forget anything, hell! If she were there he'd ask her what he looks like, eyes closed, without looking at a photograph. "What do I look like?" he wants to ask her. Because if she doesn't remember she could think he's ugly, with coarse hair, his skin a darker color, if she sees one of his brothers go by the house she could think he's the same. Sometimes he forgets what his own face looks like, but he looks at himself in the mirror and that's it.

His father's eyes are chestnut too, he looks at himself facing the mirror, he always faces things. His father looks sideways a lot, always sideways. Facing people sometimes, but not always, nothing like that. And when he's mad he looks up, when he's very upset he keeps looking up like that. So then when he's looking up he's not looking sideways anymore, he changes completely, he turns red, blue all over, he starts to turn blue from being so red, very upset, medium height, very coarse black hair, white teeth, it's incredible, to this day he doesn't have even one rotten one. He didn't have a mirror in the room at the Grand Baurú Boardinghouse, once he went running from the room to the bathroom, he couldn't stand it in that room anymore, with no mirror, he went into the bathroom to trim his beard, looking at himself in the mirror. And the mother always looks you in the face, there's nothing hidden in her look, the simple humble look of a faithful lady.

—Don't forget, you swore to tell nothing but the truth, you chickenshit son of a bitch. You could tell Gloria anything, but not me. I know you too well.

He knows people by the way they look at you, and also by the way they talk, yes? He knows when someone's telling the truth or not, when people tell the truth or are planning to lie, or trying to get him involved in some kind of a trick, his mother's look is the look of a sincere person, a look without betrayal. The father's is the look of the traitor himself, the kind who betrays whenever he has to, he's full of tricks, isn't he? But María da Gloria's look is very positive, she looks you in the face, from behind, from the left, from the right, she examines every-thing, she's a little female with a good head, and she knows how to talk well, yes? She doesn't swear. Olga was a kid back then but she always looked sideways, or down, at his fly.

—OK, let's start right there, chicken, why did you like going to a house where they laughed at you behind your back, the farm boy?

They trusted him a lot at Olga's house, he went there every night, after making out with Gloria, and he didn't want any trouble. Olga's father owned the biggest gas station in town, one of the prettiest houses, across from María da Gloria's. But once they invited him to have a beer, and another one and another one and he fell asleep until it was time to go back to the farm with his mother and Olga's two brothers came and piled blankets on top of him, almost to the ceiling, for fun, they were kids. So Olga said, "Hell, you'll kill the boy!" And this and that, and they shot out of there and she went over to that corner and kissed him on the mouth, and he pretended to be asleep. So from then on they started playing, and when no one was looking he'd hug her in some corner and give her those very tight squeezes, and an exchange of big kisses, all that stuff, but always playing, until she said, "I already know very well that Gloria and Azucena come first because they're young ladies and I'm still a child." And he said, "Hell! Then what are we going to do?" And Olga said, "Let's keep everything secret like this because my parents probably won't accept it, no way, I'm not saying it for myself because even though I'm only twelve

years old I've loved you for a long time, more than anything because of the trust they've given you in my household, do you understand what I'm saying?" But he never
wanted to meet her secretly again.

—The truth, chickenshit, liar.

Why doesn't anyone believe him? Gloria didn't want
him to leave town, Goddamnit! What else could he do?
He didn't have any clothes! What did Gloria want—for
him to go to church and get married in the raw? Working
with his father didn't settle anything because he didn't
give him anything. Free food, that was it. Breakfast, rice,
water, that kind of thing, nothing more. "Between a soccer player and a person who works the land and another
one who's a doctor or whatever, which one would be your
preferred boyfriend to marry?" "A soccer player's salary
here in Cocotá is very small, five cruzeiros, ten cruzeiros,
it doesn't pay," she said. So he, "Son of a bitch, this one
wants a millionaire!" And she said, "I'd rather you were
something like a construction worker or an electrician."
So he became both things, first he went into electrical
work and after that into civil construction. Because he
studied every morning at the school in town and he didn't
work on the farm much, the father didn't say anything to
him but the mother told him that the father told her that
he didn't work much, at five in the morning he went out
to round up the cattle from the countryside and milk
them, then he cut the cane and then he rested and at eight
he went to school, and he didn't come back to help out on
the farm, every night at Olga's house they invited him to
dinner, after that, making out with María da Gloria, and

at night he went back to the farm with the mother. The
mother told him, "After class like a good son you have to
come back to the farm, because there's always tilling,
sowing and caring for the plants to be done."

—And she got what she wanted, to separate you from
that Gloria of yours. She screwed you good, the old
whore.

—No! What's this bitch saying? Pay no attention to
her, she's mad because today he couldn't give her even
one bill.

—Who are you? I was talking to that chickenshit, to
Josemar, not to you, I don't know you.

—You don't know me? I live here in Baurú.

—I've never been to that shit town, and I don't know
who you are, stop bothering me.

—Everyone knows me here in Baurú, they say, Hello!
Good morning! when they see me go by.

—I don't talk to strangers.

—But I'm not staying here in Baurú, because when I
get enough together for that car I'm leaving.

—That Josemar isn't in Baurú anymore, and you are.
That chickenshit Josemar told me that Baurú was very
far away, all he thought about was going home, damn
chickenshit that he is.

—I am not a damn chickenshit.

—But he is, and it's lucky his neighbors over there in
Santísimo turn their radio up loud and he'll be able to
listen to some music, poor bastard, his radio doesn't have
any batteries.

—I'm in Baurú, a completely strange place, fuck. I

say to the owner of the boardinghouse, that jukebox sounds shitty as a son of a bitch.

—He was going crazy in Baurú with no friends, wasn't he? But you like it because you're not a damn chickenshit.

—Me?

—Yes, that's why you're going to stay here in Baurú forever. While that chickenshit son of a bitch is in Santísimo. If you don't want to be a chickenshit son of a bitch you have to stay in Baurú forever.

—No! I want to go home, my mother makes my food, even if it's just polenta with nothing in it, but I don't mind being poor, we have a roof over our heads and food.

—You stay there in Baurú, you don't have a house anymore, or food, and your old lady went someplace else because she's sick.

—But why are you talking to me like that? Don't you remember who I am? Don't you remember my face? What's going on here? Doesn't anyone remember anymore?

Who stayed there? But in Baurú the guy who doesn't come from there feels this coldness all over, desperation, doesn't he? But no! He's not there anymore. Where's a mirror? He doesn't know. He has to shave! With common soap like this, he doesn't have any shaving cream left, fuck it, he's all out. But the important thing is to operate the razor slowly, what's the rush, yes? So one day he had a conversation with a guy, "Hell! The situation is as follows: I'm a guy who doesn't come from around here, from Baurú, I come from another town," and that whole line of things. He planned it all himself, yes? So he went to see a game, bad enough to make you sick, wasn't it? He thought they played like shit. So he thought one day if he got up the nerve he'd go up to this guy, the one who coached the team, and tell him the following, "I'm a new ECSP employee, just hired, I'm here in Baurú taking care of the turbines, and I'd like to have a friendly word with you, sir, after paying my respects to you, and to your soccer team, which is also named Baurú, and later participate in one of your team's practices, if possible." So the guy would say to him, "OK, now that you've talked about what you propose to do, the doors are wide open; look, young man, we practice here on Wednesdays and Thursdays, beginning at three, will they give you permission at work?" He answered, "Sure they'll give it to me, and for earlier, too, if you want." Then the guy declared, "You show up at four." And he asked him exactly what position he played best, "Left forward, also halfback, and I play fantastically well, you'll see in practice, sir, I'm from such and such a town." Then the guy said, "I'm not promising you anything, but I'll pit you against that guy who played in the last game, did you see him?" So he said, "I saw the whole old thing." Then the other one, "It's between the two of you, depending on your ability to get yourself out of a jam in that position, against such and such a team, the other guy would go sit on the bench." And he said, "Agreed." He was really going crazy waiting for Wednesday, to play, because he was right there looking at the field, which had unbelievable grass. And so he showed up, yes? He arrived and everyone in the world liked him, no? The stadium was full, fantastically full. That was when he said to himself, talking to himself like crazy people do, "Agreed."

—Talking to himself like crazy people do.

So then when it was time for practice, Wednesday at three, no, at a quarter to three, he was already there, drinking a fucking soda. So the guy introduced him to a group of friends who were there and who played on the same team. The guy introduced him to everyone in the world, he showed him to everyone, "This is the new crack player on our club." But the guy duped them all, how would you say it? he conned them, "I saw this young man play a few months ago, in such and such a city, and the guy was unbelievable, he finished with the ball." Just to give him the opportunity. So all the people were in a state of suspense, so they threw up some fliers, they stuck them up on every street corner in town, they advertised: a training session will be held Wednesday at three ten, but with the names of the guys who played, all young guys. So they put his name up last of all, "This is our new hope! The brilliant new star of the team who debuts Sunday!" So everyone in the world was reading it, Josemar Ferreira, born in such and such a town, a boy of this many years old. So, fuck it! It rained people at the training session, son of a bitch! It was this full of people, and they charged to watch the training session, and a lot, five cruzeiros. So the coach realized, yes? "This crack player will bring in big money for the team." Even though he still didn't know how the new player kicked the ball, he had no idea. So when they came out of the dugout all in playing uniforms, and all that equipment, then the crack player came out—Josemar Ferreira! Josemar Ferreira! And so the whole world, "Which one is it?" "It's that one, that's the man." Very good. So the first training session, it went fantastically well, he made so many goals that they took a liking to him in that game, too bad he doesn't remember anymore how many he made, but he made loads of them, he played unbelievably well, he played ten times better than the guy who was forced to sit on the bench. So the coach announced a new program, "Friday in such and such a town, that is, this very town, we'll have a training session beginning at nine ten at night, with the participation of our new crack player."

Hell, that's when even more people showed up, discussing it with one another, some of them were asking the others, the ones who didn't have time to see the fliers, who didn't know how to read, stuff like that, the thing is, it was packed. Finally, Sunday the stadium just exploded. The game that day was against Cruzeiro de Mato Grosso. So when it was time to appear on the playing field he'd already greeted the fans. There were a lot of pretty females, rich bitches, the daughters of those guys. So he said to himself, talking to himself, "You're incredible today, if you could give it to the ball the way you did in the two training sessions . . . this will be unbelievable." So he said to the coach, "Listen, Chief, I already promised I wouldn't disappoint you, and today I won't disappoint you even if they tear me apart, with a crowd of fans like this, and I'll be the new idol in town, I'm going to play superior soccer, I won't promise to score you goals, it's a tough position, but I'll do what I can." The game began ten minutes later, one of the guys, no one knows what he did, they told someone to pass the ball to the new one, and they passed the ball to him, he dodged half the world and sent it flying into the net.

— . . .

Fucking shit! With that the people began jumping up and down and the grandstand they'd built, so more people could come, which was overloaded, began coming down. Back then they'd built it for two thousand people and there were more than ten thousand on top of that shit, and so part of it got damaged, isn't that true? So the whole world fell, people got hurt and the rest of it, but they didn't go home, nothing like that! They took care of their wounds each one as best he could, and the time went by, time went by, and after the first thirty-five minutes he went to the center of the field because the center forward had lead in his feet, he played like shit, he couldn't pass the ball either, so he took the ball from the same center forward from his own team, he dodged the defense completely and sent the ball where it had to be sent. Son of a bitch, hell! That was unbelievable. So then the crowd, everyone in the world then looked at the fliers and yelled his name which was written on it, "Josemar! Josemar! Hurray for our new glory!" Incredible, so time passed, and more time, and from that moment on his life began to change, and he forgot about all his problems from over there in that other town, María da Gloria and company. He got to know other rich bitches, several rich bitches,

he changed completely, was completely different. There
they accepted him in their homes like a son. And his three
years there were three years of triumph, and he earned a
little money from soccer, isn't that true? Sure he made
money, fucking luck turned right around, once in a while
some director of the club would come over and give him
two hundred cruzeiros, three hundred, yes? It was a lot
of money back then. So he had a little cash in his pocket
for a cold beer. Better if he had company, but if he was
alone that was even better, he didn't have to pay for some
leech of a friend or miserable whore. So what shit could
possibly matter to him, when he became the crack player
in town and had the whole world at his feet, yes? Go and
ask about him in Baurú, the whole world remembers.

Chapter Eight

It's been a while since he had a craving for fried potatoes and what he has today will make a platter of about
two pounds, more or less. Sunday's a long day and even
if a guy gets up late he has time to fuck up everyone in
the world. He thought, "If the weather's good I'll play
ball this afternoon, after the fried potatoes." Because the
mother left him a medium-size sack of potatoes, a bag of
rice, but smaller, yes? Two tomatoes half rotten already,
and a large quantity of oil. He'll see about that later because it's raining and it's not worth a damn like that. But
he'll eat the potatoes, all of them, even if they take two
hours to peel. He didn't have lunch on Thursday so he
just kept working on that fucking project, fucking kitchen
with those shitty pipes. He told the assistant, pretending,

"I don't have time, I'll stay here while you go find your soda and your piece of bread with sugar on it." Nutritious lunch, yes? But he had just enough for the return trip on the bus. And on Friday the same thing happened, he calculated the bid wrong, the cost of materials went up, he broke a pipe without realizing it, all expenses out of his pocket, fuck them. When he was working with the little black as his assistant it didn't matter if he told him the truth, this one he won't tell shit to. If the black Zilmar were here, who has less in life than he does, he'd share his potatoes. And if he eats them all now there won't be anything to eat tonight. But no one comes to the house when his mother's not there, especially with this fucking rain, who's going to find out. At least he doesn't have to water the fruit trees out back, but there isn't even one orange left. It could happen to anyone, a day or two with no gas in the tank, it's nothing to be ashamed of, if anyone knocks on his door today he's not going to open it. And tomorrow, Monday, they pay him 25 percent of the final invoice. Today he'll rest, the sun may be coming out in a while, and he'll play a good game on the mud field, even though he's got a little cold. He would open the door if the black came by, even though he always brings bad news. He wouldn't open it for a woman. Not any of them. And he'll smack the shit out of the mother of his sons if she fucks with him much. The little black was working near Baurú, that time he passed through Baurú he was hungrier than hell, "I want to tell you all about Cocotá, I've just come from there, I was just passing through same as I am here." And earlier he'd asked him, "Nigger from hell, when in your life were you hungrier?" And the black, "Many times, faggot; the worst was when I got out of the army, and I worked hardest those months, until there wasn't any more work; and I had to pay for the room, but there wasn't any work and I used up my provisions; about that time something turned up and I ate, but there was one week when nothing turned up, and one day I couldn't stand it anymore, one Saturday; I couldn't get out of bed by then, faggot; and now I'll tell you all about Cocotá." And he said better yet, he'd tell him about a certain Deusa, the one who asked him to kill her husband, but no, the black started telling him about Cocotá.

—Niggershit, who let you in here?

—I don't know who you are, I'm Zilmar.

—You'll remember me soon enough, filthy nigger! Why didn't you drink water if you were hungry?

—Don't get mad like that, sir. I did drink water, and there was a negress, Margareth, I said to her, don't you have a little extra bread? So she gave me bread and even coffee, fucking hell, that's how I lost my health! I was much stronger before, isn't that true? I never again had the body I used to have.

—Niggershit, in the countryside you ate, you played ball, yes? You worked, you climbed in through the window, you mounted the negress Teresa, what the fuck did you leave the countryside for?

—Because they called me into the army, sir, and after that I stayed in fucking Rio. Who are you, sir?

—You still don't recognize me?

—I don't know, sir, you haven't shaved, you haven't taken a bath, you smell like hell, and with the windows closed and the door, too, so no one can see that you have nothing left but a sack of potatoes, it's very dark in here.

—I have four pounds of potatoes, I won't go hungry while others do, worthless nigger. You're already used to going to bed without eating.

—Yes sir, you're right, but I never got used to going to bed without eating. If Josemar doesn't share anything with me tonight and I go to bed hungry I'll go to sleep and wake up again, I won't be able to sleep, I'll go to sleep and wake up again.

—Fuck yourself and shut up, shit! And go check that door, see if it's shut tight, and the window, check the window bar so no one comes in here today. Shitty women.

—Everything's shut tight, sir.

—Could you mount your negress from hell when you weren't eating?

—It's possible to give her one ride, just one; no more than that, no matter how much you want to, and the woman has to be the type you prefer. If not, impossible, you can't manage a damn thing.

—And Josemar? What the fuck does he do with females on an empty stomach?

—He told me the same thing happens to him, sir, with a full belly it's one thing, if not, it's another; a person is so weak that he falls on top of the female, bang-bang-bang, in two minutes it's over; because a person's weak, he can't control himself, because if a person make a big effort he fucks up his lungs; without eating if he screws a female in two or three days he gets sick in the lungs; without eating he starts to sweat, and even so he keeps thinking of banging somebody.

—Niggershit, you don't have to be a coward, you chickenshit, tell the whole truth.

—Yes, sir, I'm telling you. If his body isn't ready a person thinks about it but then he gives it up. Me, one time I was eating bad, working and eating bad, understand? I'd skip lunch, I'd skip dinner, if I had dinner I didn't have anything for lunch, and I was screwing this female. She'd come to the room I was renting so I'd screw her, and one day she'd come and one day she wouldn't, and one day she came and stayed, we screwed all day, didn't we? She was single but we didn't feed ourselves; and the day came when I started shaking so badly that I kept on shaking for like two hours; and in a cold sweat; a lot of days I'd been screwing her two and three times a day; always at night, I'd get there, take a bath, have dinner and we'd start.

—Fucking nigger, I can screw just as much, even if I don't eat! But what happens to me is it takes longer to shoot my wad, or I can't shoot it, I'm different, but the flag flies high.

—I told Josemar, "Fucking faggot, you have to make a woman enjoy it," make her come two or three times while under your piston, yes? At least once, twice, if possible; but if the guy is weak he finishes right away and you have to know how to get her ready so you can finish with her at the same time, if not, where's the big man? It's no good if the woman comes first and the guy later, she won't get pregnant if they don't finish at the same time; if they finish together she has to take the pill, if not she can save it; I know what it's like to sleep with a woman and be hungry; she, hungry too, Hell! Even though it was night, that Thursday we didn't do anything; I told her, "No screwing if we don't want to get sick," they pay me on Saturdays, and Fridays she worked as a servant but she hadn't eaten that day and she got to my room hungry too, so she took all the change I had, I don't remember how much it was, I know it was some tiny amount; so then she went and bought a piece of bread, one of those with sugar on it. She ate one piece and I ate the other; but no screwing, what shit, no? You understand.

—Understand what? I don't know what that tiny amount is, that's why I'm asking you, you lousy nigger.

—I'm telling you sir. So on Saturday I went to the company, I picked up the cash, then I came back, did the shopping, around two in the afternoon, and then I made dinner; she'd gone to work, later she came back.

—But this four-pound plate of fried potatoes, this you too would have craved.

—I bought meat, fruit, didn't I? Eggs, a good beefsteak, bread, an egg on top of the steak. She and I, son of a bitch! We had some Coca Cola; then we rested a little, from so much lunch; so when we woke up it was six in the afternoon, we lazed around about a little, took a bath and started to make up for the day we hadn't had any food; it's no joke, no; people, a man, especially, has to try and feed himself really well, if not the saber falls, and one time I had to work on a house that was on the beach, far from everything, in Saquarema, the State of Rio, hell! next to Cabo Frío. I went to work over there, my friend, with that fresh ocean air, yes?

—I'm not your friend.

—Excuse me, sir, and they made dinner there for all the employees because they had to be there really far from everything, and I put on eight pounds in the twenty days I was working there; we ate everything, we swam in the ocean early in the morning, and at noon there was lunch, and it was all like that; and the foreman told me what I had to do to be a member of it, of the union. But you'd better throw the potatoes on, all of them, the oil is sizzling, isn't it? It would be best for you to leave half for tonight, don't share them with me.

—I was in the union before, too, but now I'm nonunion and it's the same thing, if I break an arm they pay for the hospital, and who do you think you are? You starvation case.

—But you, sir, as nonunion you don't have vacations or a damn thing, if you stop working it's your problem. And you're an electrician, a mason, a carpenter, a plumber, and a painter all at once, and the union doesn't make them pay you for each one of them, because a specialist has a minumum salary, but the union doesn't make them pay you for each one of the specialties, not one shit.

—Shut up, asshole! The worst thing of all is to give a client an estimate for less than it's going to be, yes? And the client starts in with how it's very expensive, you're robbing me, you're a son of a bitch, and the guy who

wants to work ends up cutting the price and then he goes
and the cost of materials went up, cement didn't go up, is
that right or not? But every brick went up almost double
and, after that, cement did too, and by the time he's ready
to hand over the finished product sometimes he ends up
losing and has to take it out of his own pocket.

—And the poor guy's head begins to buzz from nerves,
his life is ruined, not even a broad does him any good,
Josemar told me that when he's nervous he doesn't feel a
thing, it's like giving an injection, nerves ruin everything, yes? Because the head controls the member, the
club, which isn't a club when you're upset.

—That happens to niggers from hell, not me.

—That guy from the job at the beach began talking to
me about how when I got back to Rio he had to put me in
touch with other masons because the union is the power
and ends the exploitation of poor people. And I went, the
police even broke us up, for contempt of the government.

—In Baurú I'm unionized, what kind of shit do you
believe? And I don't have anything against this government now, but it seems wrong as hell to me; if I was in
the government I'd lower the cost of living, I'd lower fuel,
so that people could go in cars as much as they wanted,
and I'd make bus fares really low. And I'd take better
care of the city, especially the towns in the interior, because it's really wrong, raising the price of fuel twice a
month.

—You haven't even got a car and you still don't agree.
But just the same, wouldn't you want everyone in the
world to have the same things?

—Idiot! Of course, but that can never be, there have to be people who are poorer people and people who are richer. There are people who don't have enough to eat and others who serve themselves almost four pounds of fried potatoes and don't leave even one as a souvenir. Yes, in Communist countries they say they can, but not here. It's not possible here, because if all the people were on the same level then no one would work. But that's too much for an ignorant nigger to understand—like you!

—Yes sir.

—I think: but there have to be people with much better lives so that they can give other people work. If not they wouldn't have work. And here in Rio if the assistant who works with me was rich he wouldn't work with me, yes? He'd work for his own business. So since I'm luckier than he is, in spite of not being rich, I help him, I help a whole family don't I?

—Sir, you're somebody of a higher category.

—What's this about category? A damn chickenshit, that's what he is, and start helping your own family, before other people's, liar from hell!

—Who's that woman, sir?

—A street bitch.

—OK, sir, then I won't pay any attention to her, now I'll tell you all about Cocotá, because I have a lot of new things to tell you, about María da Gloria, it seems that . . .

—Later! I'll tell you things about here in Baurú.

—You chickenshit, you're not in Baurú now, you're here, in Santísimo, and you have two kids who have to eat every day.

—You can tell me about Cocotá another day, there's no rush, right?

But first Josemar will tell him something, something completely true. It turns out that one Wednesday he didn't have to work and he met someone in the street who he'd traveled on the bus with from São Paulo to here in Baurú, a long trip, and she said she was staying at her sister-in-law's house and he walked her to the house and when they arrived the sister-in-law opened the front door and it was that Deusa woman, he was always running into her in the street and she would always look at him, even though she was walking arm in arm with her husband, who was a truck driver. But Josemar is a decent person, and María da Gloria doesn't know that, one day he's going to tell her.

—Chickenshit, don't forget to tell her you stole a thousand cruzeiros from a poor old man who gave you a steak.

—And at first he went out with the younger one but that Deusa started to like him too, yes? The two of them. But the younger one went back to São Paulo, and she wrote him once and she sent him a message for the sister-in-law. He got there around noon, Deusa opened the door, her husband was arriving at two in the afternoon. "Here's the letter they sent me to give you." So one thing leads to another and Deusa goes and asks him a question, "Did you screw my sister-in-law, or what?" And she also told him that her husband would only arrive at two-fifteen. And he, "No, nothing's happened yet, I didn't give it to her." So Deusa said something like this, "That's not

1 3 5

possible." So the following happened: In that same period of time the business with the two of them started, he
screwed her in the bathroom standing up, the guy's wife,
the truck driver's. So they started, and whenever the
husband left on a trip he mounted her, he never missed
even one opportunity. So one day there was a bus crash,
near Parada de Lucas, on the road to São Paulo, and no
one knew anything more, so she said to him something
like this, "I shit on him! Can it be that son of a bitch who
died?" He said, "I don't know." So right away on the
radio they announced that it wasn't the guy. So she told
him she wanted to have him killed, "Because of you I'm
going to have him killed, so we can live together, so I can
live with an unbelievable man, yes?" And he always gave
her the same response, "You're not going to do anything
of the kind, he's an honest, hardworking man, he has to
live, isn't that so?"

—If they paid you a hundred thousand cruzeiros
you'd kill him. From behind, you chickenshit.

—But I have a lot more to tell you about Cocotá,
about . . .

Wait a minute! It's that she was very bad tempered,
she fought with her husband a lot, and she really hated
him, she didn't love her husband at all, not at all. She
said she hated him because her husband mounted her and
she didn't feel anything, no matter how much she yearned
for it. And time passed and her husband got worse every
time because finally he couldn't raise his flag at all and
he couldn't mount her, and she was going wild for the
other guy. And the husband tried remedies but the prob-

lem continued, and she wanted to have him killed, she had already decided. But then he stopped seeing Deusa, who was a real dish, a shameless female straight out of hell.

—Josemar, faggot, aren't you going to let me get a word in edgewise? It's about Gloria!

And if the little black came to Santísimo today to say hello to his mother, who brought him up when he was left an orphan, he wouldn't find her, but he'd tell the black chimp about someone else who was dangerous as hell, but she's from Copacabana, loaded with cash, an old bag, a veteran from you know what. And if he doesn't believe him he can go to hell. The one he's not going to tell him about is the teacher from Cocotá, Valseí. Because a man who's a gentleman can't say anything about a woman that will stain her reputation. And if anyone came to visit at this moment and saw him with this plate of fried potatoes the guy would know what an abundant plate is. The one from Copacabana was a doctor's wife, and once in a while she'd tell him, "I'm going to have my husband killed so I can live with my love." She always said the same thing. He changed all the kitchen tiles, and she liked his work a lot, and she liked the mason a lot, too. So she abandoned herself totally to him, she lived to call him, for a beer, for lunch, for dinner together, is that clear? So everything's in order, no problems, and the day came when it was time to give her the club number. So one day he made a date with the veteran, he said to her, "The situation is as follows: We meet at ten tonight." So they went out at ten and went to a hotel far from Copaca-

bana, and they stayed there all night and came back at
six in the morning. He didn't know her husband. She said
to him, "Oh, poor me, I have to have him killed, he's
living with another woman." Her husband, but the guy
lives and sleeps in her house, the veteran, she's older than
he is, he lives with one and the other one, is that clear?
She owns three apartments, that lady. So she told him she
couldn't stand her relationship with her husband, it's
been more than five years since he touched her, but he
doesn't let her go out and sleep around. Because they
have two children, his and hers, yes? He was a poor boy
and she made him rich, no? She made him study, she
gave him money to get his medical degree, and after he
got it he abandoned her, son of a bitch! Once in a while
she felt the urge for a nice club, delivered with flavor.
And if she wanted to he'd go to a hotel with her. And in
the hotel one time just at the moment he was mounting
her she fell off the bed, she hurt her head and so did he,
but not as bad. She fell off the bed at the final toast and
without realizing it she stuck her head between the bars
of the headboard and she started bleeding, and she said,
"If you won't promise me you'll kill him . . . I'll call the
police and tell them you hurt me on purpose." And he
didn't pay attention to her and that was the last time.

—You were waiting for her to offer you a million
cruzeiros, but she didn't talk about dough. You chickenshit, son of a bitch.

The black wouldn't believe him, sometimes he doesn't
tell him things because the black doesn't believe anything. The black told him, "A negress wanted to kill me

and herself!" in Rio, a servant in the Leme neighborhood, "I didn't know she was sick in the head and I
mounted her, luckily I didn't see her again, because she
always wore white, she was upset because she'd had a
guy's child and she was single, and she wanted to suffo-
cate the child with a pillow, and then she'd repent and go
screaming to the police station."

—She didn't claw herself with her nails like I did?
What did she scream?

"She screamed that her life was hell on earth. And
when she fought with me she screamed the same thing at
me, that, that her life was hell on earth. She'd go to the
police station, if someone couldn't stop her, to turn herself in as guilty of a crime, of killing her child; and her
employer found her in the street, the lunatic had gone out
with the child wrapped up in a rag and she was in the
middle of the street so the cars would run her over." He
doesn't believe everything the black tells him about
Cocotá, that they sent him their regards, and that he'd
asked about him, that man, the landowner, and that he'd
told him to say that if he came back to town he should
come by and say hello, and that he should see the soccer
field they'd built behind the house, and the tennis court,
and that he was happy that a boy from that town was
working well outside, even though he was an ingrate because he'd left without saying good-bye. And that the
landowner's sons are grown up already, and they're starting to go out with girls, and he didn't tell the black about
the schoolteacher. Something like fifteen years had passed
when he ran into her.

—Sir, these potatoes are so nice and crispy, don't they burn your mouth this hot?

He did all of elementary school with her, there was no other teacher. That was good because he loved her a lot. Later she disappeared, the earth swallowed her up. And he was twenty-seven years old already when they sent him to do an inspection of a line near Mato Grosso, right? So he recognized her, he approached her, he looked at her for quite a while. He was staying at the Porto Hotel, in that place, working for ECSP, he always saw her go by at eight-thirty in the morning, fine, he told himself, "That's Valseí, it has to be her." He was leaning out the window of his room. So one day he came down from his room and walked over to her, "Pardon me, ma'am excuse me for what I'm about to say, don't misunderstand, but your name is Valseí, isn't that true?", "My name is Valseí Ribeiro, it's true my name is Valseí." So he said to her, "Where did you used to live? What years did you teach classes in other towns?" "I taught in Cocotá, I taught in Nova Iguaçú, I taught in Miguel Couto," "And do you remember some of your students?" "Yes, I remember many students," "And don't you remember a pretty strange tale that had to do with a student who was lazier than shit?" So she thought and thought, and he tried to put her on the right track, "Look, son, the situation is as follows: I've had a lot of students, and I'm very happy that you came over to talk to me, but I'm late. Let's do the following: We'll meet right here later on, at eight tonight, and we'll see what each of us remembers; but tell me, what do you do?" "I'm a line supervisor for

ECSP." She already knew the company. And he said that most of all he was a transformer adjustor. But it was very clear that she still didn't remember who he was. She was still pretty. A well-shaped body. And he told her, "Don't be late, Miss, I'll be here at eight, I'll be done with dinner already; and don't leave me waiting, there's one detail that's going to be kind of a surprise." And so at eight on the dot she appeared. He saw her from the window of his hotel room. He said, "Let's talk, yes? Let's go sit in that square," and she talked about some students who were friends of his back then, but she didn't say anything about him, "Listen, I had some very naughty students, very rebellious, one was Geraldo, he was really a lot of work, he was always getting into some mess; there was that Geraldo, Léo, Cleó, Doraldo, a bunch of very rowdy little boys, I remember them well." And later she asked him to walk her home, it was far and it was late already, down some dark streets, and so she said to him, "I feel better with a man escorting me at this hour, it's so dark out; I never go out at this hour because I'm afraid to go home alone; I like the life of a single woman, but this I really don't like, not having someone to walk me home at night." And he couldn't stand it and he took her by the arm. She asked him what day he was born and then she said his star sign was very special, the lion's sign. And as they were passing some very thick trees, he stopped and said that those were like the ones in Cocotá, and it wasn't true, to see what she'd say, if she wanted to keep walking home fast or if she'd stay there. She stood there like a tame cow. And he mounted her on the grass, he doesn't even remember what it was like, all he remembers is that they didn't speak, practically, that he hugged her and she didn't put up a fight, he took off her panties and put her on the grass and made her yell with pleasure, but then he said good-bye right there, he didn't walk her home because he told her something or other, that they were waiting for him to play a game of billiards or something like that, and he made a date with her for the next night, and he doesn't remember if he had to go inspect some line in the country or what, or if he had to go back to Baurú the next day, already, but he never did see her again. He didn't say anything to her about that letter he wrote her when he was eleven years old, why waste time? She wouldn't remember him anyway, when a woman's a whore it doesn't make any difference if it's one guy or another. Even though he thought she was a different class of woman, yes? But he didn't tell that to the black. And why leave these four or five potatoes on the plate? Down the hatch!

Chapter Nine

—Why is the house so clean?

His mother came back, she's a very good lady and
right away she started cleaning everything up.

—It's been a long time since you've thought about me,
hasn't it?

But she didn't come back cured. They told her the
same thing in the hospital in Cocota as they did in the one
in Santísimo, "Ma'am, you have to take a treatment and
you have to stay in this town so your oldest daughter can
care for you." He asked her, "Then why did you come
back, old girl, if you haven't finished the treatment that
will cure you, and completely?" And she, "Your oldest
sister will take care of me and I'll be completely cured,
thanks to my son who paid for the operation last year,

which turned out so expensive, I owe everything to him, to this son who's so good." And she gave him a big hug. But crying from sadness, not from happiness.

—Wasn't she grateful to God that she was going to get well?

She was upset, the treatment that they told her in Santísimo was very expensive, they told her in Cocotá it was going to be even more expensive. And the old lady, "All I have to sell is this house, but if I do that, you'll be left without a roof over your head, my beloved son who saved my life; and never in my life will I let that happen." And he remained in a corner thinking, "Don't worry, old girl, your son is going to get that fucking money, and if not you can sell the house with peace of mind, because your son is a man now." But he was very sad. Even though he's going to get it, that money, and without selling the house, isn't that true?

—Your mother's asleep, why did you wake up? It's barely two in the morning.

If Gloria would listen to him he'd ask her for one thing.

—What? I'm listening.

For a sign, whatever it may be, yes? That she still loves him.

—Why?

He's never been so screwed in his life and he's asking her to help him. If the mother realized what's happening to him, fuck, she'd get even sicker and die.

—And the little son will be left all alone—chickenshit! What are you thinking? That ball that belongs to your children is deflated, you can't play with it.

The ball has a flat inner tube. When he got home from work she was visiting, the mother of his children. He treated her well, because they're not on speaking terms and that kind of stuff, but when he got home he found the mother talking to that woman. And she, "Will you give me permission to visit your mother?" And he, "OK, no problem, you have the blessing of this house, as far as I'm concerned you can stay as long as you want," because she was with the two boys. The ball has a flat inner tube and they left it with him to fix. So he went out, he went to take a bath and that kind of thing, then he went to heat up dinner, to eat whatever there was, he was dying of hunger, he hadn't even had lunch. And later when that fucking María Lourdes went out, in the street she said, "Are you satisfied with my coming here?" And he, "Your coming is justified because you're seeing the old lady." And she offered to help her as much as possible during her illness. Then he said, "I'm grateful to you, I consent, and if it were possible, if I had the money, I'd pay you because I'm needing the help." And she, "Always so proud, aren't you? You want to pay for everything." And he, "No, it's not that, it's that I don't like owing anyone favors." And she carried off the two children, who were being a nuisance, fighting in front of the grandmother, and she carried them off. He gave them a kiss and they asked him for a hundred cruzeiros to fix the ball, he didn't have it. He said, "Too bad I don't have it, another day, yes, but today I don't have a cent," "Oh, because we want to play," and this and that, "OK, calm down, this weekend I'll give it back to you retreaded. I'll keep the ball and tomorrow I'll take it to a place where they'll fix it for me without charging me anything." "Papa! Why don't you give us ten cruzeiros for sweets?" "Yes, Papa, give us those ten cruzeiros! Don't be bad!" And then he, "I don't have it today, it's all gone, I have just enough for the bus to work tomorrow, not a cent more, I swear." And the bigger one, "OK, then Saturday we'll come and get the ball." And he, "Then Saturday you'll come over and get the ball." And the fucking Lourdes said good-bye to his mother, "Ma'am, I'll try and help you in my free time, I'll come over whenever I can," and she chatted like that a little longer, she's a very worthy woman.

—I don't care what you think of me anymore, I know you too well already.

One is six years old, the other's four, the most rebellious of the two, and they're together all day. She says they fight, break everything, throw everything on the floor, they make a big ruckus in the household. They're both handsome. And she's a very educated woman, she talked a lot, she laid her cards on the table. And he, "What a long visit you had, old girl." And the mother spoke to him like this, "That's OK, she's good to me, but it's the father of the children who she doesn't love at all." And he said, "What I wanted was two sons and now I have them." And he dropped the subject, he went out to the backyard. The mother of his sons will come over to help, she'll do the laundry, when he's not there, and she asked the old lady why she was going back to town, "Why don't you want to keep living here, ma'am?" And

the old lady, "Because I might sell the house and stuff
like that." And the other, "And where's your son going
to stay?" And the old lady, "He'll look after himself."
And the other, "But that's a pretty strange business, isn't
it?" The fucking Lourdes didn't like the business, she
didn't like it at all, not one bit. And the mother, "If I sell
it's because I'll be forced to because I have this health
problem and I have to take good care of it; don't say anything to Josemar, but I also have a Social Security debt
to pay, so I have to put all of this in order." And that's
how her visit went long as a poor man's hope. And she
said she'll always come back, to help the old lady, when
she has laundry to do and that kind of thing.

—If they take your roof away from you don't come
looking for me, because you're not setting foot in the
house of me and my children.

She's a teacher and she works double shifts, he thinks
she starts at eight at one school and she leaves at noon,
and from two on she's in a private school. Her life is like
that, she works harder than hell. And later at home she
has to finish the rest of it, with her kids, make dinner, the
milk, the bottle, the whole business with kids. She's a
virtuous woman, a hard worker. But it's been four years
now since he's touched her, and he has no desire at all.
When he gets sick of something it's for good, isn't that
true? When he says he's had enough, he doesn't want any
more, it's over. He doesn't look back. Once he's out he
doesn't go back in.

—Because the door is shut.

She argued a lot with him, didn't she? And he, hell!

He doesn't have the time, not even a fixed schedule of when he comes home, he never knows what time he can leave the work under construction, and even so she wanted to control his schedule, it's true that it was like that. She'd say, "I'll expect you home by seven tonight without fail." Every day. Hell, not him. He wasn't going to play that game, was he? How could he be back early every day, home by seven? What time would he quit work? Some nights he went to sleep with her, others he went to his house.

—You never threw a snake on top of her, like you did me, to scare me?

She and snakes play on the same team. But she's not ugly, quite pretty, white with long black hair. Now she's dyed it blonde, the landscape's changed, mean like hell! She and a snake could live together, they'd have fun, they're both wild beasts.

—You never thought about killing her, like a snake?

He thought that if he saw María da Gloria with someone else he'd kill her. The black, Zilmar, that time he passed through Baurú he told him, "María da Gloria is better, she's gone back to school now, if she can finish her studies she'll get her teaching degree one day; her nerves are better now. She doesn't think about what happened. But she rarely goes out, she doesn't have a boyfriend, that I'm sure of."

—That's not true, I keep thinking about what happened.

And he said to the black, "What you said isn't true, she keeps thinking about what happened." And the black

asked him why he'd never made friends with Matías.
And it's true, Matías wasn't a friend of his, but Gloria
talked a lot with this Matías, his name was Matías, that
guy, a tall, fat guy. So she always said the same thing,
"Matías was brought up in this house, along with my
brother, I don't have anything to do with Matías." But
for him it was a war of nerves.

—Matías went to study and I never saw him again.

Hell, he told her not to talk to the guy anymore! He
saw that the guy liked her a little. Matías went to college,
and he got a degree in one of those things, agronomy,
"Hell, I don't want to see you talking to that guy anymore!" But you can't yell at María da Gloria too much
because she's sick. They told him she sees him even
though he's far away, doesn't she? She sees him coming
with a bouquet of flowers, bigger each time, they say.

—That's true, I don't forget, I keep thinking about
what happened. And don't be sad, your mother went out
to water the fruit trees and you're not in Baurú anymore.

—You chickenshit, nothing like that, don't take advantage of that poor crazy girl because she believes
everything you say, you have to tell the truth even if it
fucks you up.

He'd gone to put up some poles, the high-tension ones,
in the countryside, but when he got back to Baurú they
advised him that personnel had moved without notice.
ECSP wasn't there anymore, is that clear? And he didn't
have even one cent in his pocket, or almost nothing, two
cruzeiros. They'd moved, all the personnel, the boardinghouse was left for shit, and everyone had gone to another

town almost as far as Mato Grosso, which was about five
hundred miles, and he didn't have a cent to travel with.
Because he was alone in that town, yes? With no one to
ask for help, not one colleague had stayed behind, they'd
left him the address to go to in the hotel and nothing else.
He wasn't close friends with anyone, he hadn't been there
long. He'd spent three years in Baurú and now he had to
leave. For more than two hours he thought about how he
was going to get to Mato Grosso without a cent. Then he
started planning how to pull a fast one on somebody,
later on he went over to the guy's boardinghouse, "You
know that I'm from here, I've been here a long time and
all that, I need twenty cruzeiros to get to a town near
Mato Grosso; and I'll be back on such and such a day to
return your money." The guy didn't have the cash and he
was just waiting for the bus to leave, he wasn't feeling
too well deep in his guts at that moment, when the bus
was about to leave, it was going to leave at eleven-forty;
he took the bus then and said good-bye to everyone in
town, including the ones he played soccer with, no more
problems now. Three years there in Baurú, then the bus
left, but he wasn't close friends enough to anyone to
borrow money or stuff like that, is that clear? Because he
didn't have any family in Baurú, and he was starting to
go crazy, who was he going to ask? Then he spoke to that
guy, and the guy said, "With pleasure, no problem." He
proposed pawning a watch he had to the guy, "You keep
the watch." So the guy said, "No, no, you're an honest
young man, very nice, you never did anything wrong in
this town that I know of, but it would be better if you left

me something, I'd appreciate it." It was a gold watch, but only plated, what the fuck! So he left for the other town, over there by Mato Grosso. It was the owner of the boardinghouse, where everyone ate lunch and dinner. Everything was in order. So he left, now he'd freed himself from any obligations in the town, and another night in the bus, yes? Everything dark, everything black, you couldn't see shit.

—I know the color black makes you sad.

For him the color black of night stands for mourning, which is when a person is very sick, about to die, or is going to give birth and could die, or the woman is dead already. When he's sad the color black stands for mourning, and when he's all right it stands for when it's time to go to sleep, time to rest. But one time, when he couldn't sleep, when the mother was complaining about the pain when she was giving birth to Vilma, he got up and wrote a letter to his teacher.

—Why is black the color of mourning? I don't know, I asked my mother and she doesn't know either.

He knows, it's something that comes from older times, yes? The slaves, and all that stuff, when Brazil was liberated, the black Brazilian people. The blacks didn't have the opportunities then that they have now, isn't that true? To walk the street, go around the countryside, and this and that, they walked around in chains, with a rope around their necks, when they did something strange or they wanted to mount a woman they killed them, and that kind of thing. Generally the blacks don't like mourning, it reminds them of when they were slaves and when they talk about Princess Isabel they start trembling all over. She was the one who freed them. But if his mother goes and sells the house he doesn't know where he'll end up.

—Your mother's sleeping soundly, wouldn't you like to go out to the garden with me? Because if you get worked up so hard like that when you cry she might wake up.

If a man is a man he doesn't cry, and he'll get a hold of himself.

—We'll go out, the air will make you feel better, there's no moon and it's very dark out.

He always asked Gloria why she liked black clothes. She wouldn't say. But one day she said, "The first time I saw you you were in black, all in black; I like a guy dressed in black." So, what the fuck, he got mad, "Now you're saying that you like a guy who wears black, what's this business? Is it me dressed in black or any guy in black?" So she, "No, I've always liked the color black, from the first moment I met you, and saw you in black, so I'm going to ask you a favor, that you always wear something black when you go out with me." So generally the two of them would go around, him in black pants or a black shirt, and her in black shoes or black jeans, there was always something black between the two of them. That's the way it was, the two of them planned it.

—Men don't cry, I like it like that, you should know how to take it. An upright man. Tonight the stars aren't shining much, are they?

There's one hour when the sky is most beautiful, at this hour, between two and three in the morning. But when the sky is clear, clear, a person looks and the sky is completely different, people who really pay attention to the sky, yes? He really pays a lot of attention; now and then he's here at dawn looking at the sky. It was last week, he woke up like today at this hour more or less. He went out to the backyard and looked up, the moon was getting round like that, that half-moon, beautiful! beautiful! Opening up like a flower, yes? Beginning to open up. Tonight it's dark and he didn't ask the mother how María da Gloria was, if she'd heard anything about her.

—It's true, what they used to say.

They said a lot of things about her, because she believed she had a child and when no one was watching she suffocated it with a pillow and later she repented and was going to the police station if they didn't catch her, to turn herself in as guilty of a crime, of killing her child. And her mother met him in the street the only time he came back to town and told him, "My daughter's life is hell on earth," because one day she wrapped something in some rags and took it in her arms like a child and crossed the street just when a car was coming so it would run her down, her and the child.

—That was something that happened to someone else, not to me. What is hell on earth?

When they were making out in the garden Gloria always asked him questions, what was his favorite thing in the world? and stuff like that, and meanwhile time went by and he was groping her as much as he wanted. But she never asked him what was hell on earth, because then he would have answered her and now she would remember. Now he can't say what it is, and in life it's important to know where the bad is so you don't take the road. If she could listen to him he'd ask her a lot of questions, too, and in this way the darkest hours of the night would pass.

—And for your mama, what would hell on earth be?

For her, heaven would be to live forever with her son, so when she was discussing it with him tonight she said, "Heck . . . I don't know what to do." And he, "You take care of your health, just sell the house." Because the house is in her name. He's the kind of son she always wanted. But he wouldn't want a rebellious child, who fights, isn't that true? So that's one thing he wouldn't want, he wouldn't accept him as his child. Because there are very good kids, you can control them by talking to them and things like that, but there are stubborn children, high-strung, who fight, throw rocks, swear, who don't love anyone, and that's one thing he wouldn't like. For him that could be hell on earth. He doesn't know.

—What's it like, hell on earth? Is there a lot of fire? Very tall bonfires?

No, there's nothing, he doesn't see any of that. He doesn't know about these things. He likes bonfires.

—Is it that you don't see anything because there's no moon and it's very dark?

It's getting cold and he thinks that tonight there must be very poor people who are sleeping outside, out in the open. If it rains the bonfires go out and the people shiver from the cold, with no roof over their heads.

—Your children aren't mine, are they? Sometimes

they turn out rebellious because the father isn't good, isn't it like that?

They were born rebellious, they were born with bad hearts, and they're impossible to hold down, you have to hit them and hitting them is useless, they get even more rebellious. They are bums from birth, they are born to steal and when they're born that way for no reason, nothing makes them happy. No matter how many presents he gives them, it's useless, their heart's already like that.

—What does that son of yours have inside his heart? Not my blood, yes?

Bad blood, not like blood that came from a person, yes? Sometimes a lion is easier to tame than a child, no? Because a lion is the following: If someone takes care of it, every day, that same person every day, the lion will become attached to the guy, but it's traitorous affection, isn't that true? It could attack him from behind, betray him from one moment to the next.

—But don't they say that the lion's the noblest animal in the jungle?

It's not true, it's one of the worst beasts that exists, he knows.

—But your sign is the sign of the lion.

But his sign is a calm lion, isn't it? He is more responsible with his two sons than his father was in his whole fucking life. His father never did anything, hell, he never helped him. When did he put on his first pair of shoes? At twelve years old, before then he had to walk barefoot, yes? Now, even with his string of bad luck and everything, whenever he can he gives what he has to his two sons, and when he has a thousand cruzeiros in his pocket he says to them, "Hey, here's cash, for shoes for the kids," and stuff like that. So his sons are well dressed, handsome, completely clean, and to him that's what it means to be a real father. The father who brings a son into the world and abandons him isn't a father, he isn't a good father.

—Are you feeling cold, is the dawn too chilly?

He's going inside because he's already caught a cold and he catches colds from nothing. He can't stand those towns any longer, colder than hell, way out, far away from everything, fucking ECSP, that's why he left that job. Out there by Mato Grosso he put up with it for about two more months, because he didn't have much time till his vacation.

—I know that soon they're going to give you a vacation there in Mato Grosso. What are you going to do those days?

And he, back then, he said to the black Zilmar that he'd also thought she's forgotten him, but it wasn't true. When he'd got his vacation from ECSP he'd go to see her, because he was going half crazy already, wasn't he? From wanting to see her.

—Let's go in, it's not good for you to feel cold.

That time he said to the black, "When I get my vacation from ECSP I'm going to see her, because I'm going half crazy already, aren't I? From wanting to see her."

—Are you going to come?

Yes, he promises on his word as a man, an upright man.

Chapter Ten

—Why are you looking at everything like that, had you forgotten what your town was like?

He didn't remember that Cocotá was a small town like this, and that the people were so poor. All the people know each other and everyone talks to everyone else. It's a town that's divided in two, yes? It has a right side and a left side and a river about a hundred meters wide that goes down the middle.

—What's wrong with you? Why are you looking at everyone out of the corner of your eye?

A river with a lot of fish, and a lot of ferocious animals, alligators are the worst. And there are tapirs like wild hogs, with those big snouts, every time it looks it opens its eyes wide. And in August it attacks, because

it's with young. It eats any kind of animal, it catches hens
to take to its young. It catches cats, and dogs, even, and
if a person is careless it catches him too.

—Did you remember that the left side is where the
better homes are?

Yes, with the church, and the river promenade, and a
very good bar, and one of the finest restaurants, and a
hotel that's also of high quality. Only one hotel, but very
clean outside, he hasn't been inside. And on the right
there are more inhabitants, with some hills where the
poorest people come together to live, Kerosén Hill and
Santa Fátima Hill. Each hill has it's name. And unpaved
streets, but well cobbled, and some dirt roads, too. And
three miles away is the farm. Half an hour walking
leisurely. You have to cross over two rivers, but narrow
ones. And with bridges and a new viaduct that he hadn't
seen. And the bus got in at five in the morning and he
walked to the farm to take a shower, yes? And a son
of a bitch of a shave. Because that afternoon he was going
to make his entrance in town, one hell of a grand entrance
in town. He was going to leave the farm, cross through a
cornfield, through sugarcane fields, pass the waterfalls, a
river, the other river, one of them has pretty rocks, and
that whole grove. He left the farm when the sun wasn't
too hot yet, so he wouldn't arrive all sweaty, and if he was
lucky and the wind didn't come up on the road, when he
got there, his hair would be clean, just like people from
town. And they start playing requests in the park at six
every Thursday. And if her nerves are cured now they'll

talk about a lot of things, her going there to Mato Grosso with him, running away with him.

—Once you said something to me that I liked a lot. If you could tell me again it would make me very happy.

He'd say a lot of things when he didn't know her yet, when he saw her go by, he'd say, "Hell! I want that rose for a pretty vase."

—No, it wasn't that. Something else, you told me right near here, where your father planted corn.

What could it have been? He promised to marry her right away, but he couldn't.

—That I know already, that you couldn't. But it was something else you said.

One Sunday in the afternoon when he'd played soccer, he'd already taken a bath and he was chatting in the square with some of his buddies: How did the game go? Who played well and who played badly? And she went by and he said to himself, "Today I'm going to let her pass, because you don't chase a tame hen." But then he looked at her and couldn't stand it and he went over and said to her, "My garden needs your flowers." And a few days went by and she passed by and she was the one who said to him, "My garden also needs your flowers." Because since she was just a kid she wasn't experienced yet in making up those kinds of words to please someone. And he answered, "Where are you going to plant those flowers?" And she, "Right at the door of my house." And he said, "Not me, I want to plant them at the door of my heart." That kind of chatter.

—No, it was something else you said to me, and I'm sure you've forgotten.

He doesn't remember. But he's not going to confess that to her because if she realizes . . . then she'll find out about everything.

—What is it I'll find out?

That he's less than she is. It is something she never has to know about.

—In what sense less than I am?

His head doesn't even work well enough to remember what it was he said to her one time and that she liked. Because he didn't study, and his brain isn't developed. He remembers things she said to him, he does remember that.

—But now you've come to Cocotá on vacation and your memories will all come back. The music has started in the park, they're putting on the records the people are requesting.

He was getting closer to the park, he could hear the music from a block away, he went into a bar and asked for a glass straight from hell, the strongest stuff they had, so his hands wouldn't shake. If someone asked for the record "Leaves," he'd know she was there, in the park. A guy announced the record on the loudspeaker and told who requested it, but just the initial, and said it was dedicated to so-and-so, but they didn't even give the initial—for the boy with the yellow shirt, they said. But he was wearing a black shirt. It doesn't matter, he drank, he warmed his balls up, and went out the door of the bar to hear the music better, he couldn't hear anything, they were changing the record or the loudspeaker was broken. No, they were changing the record, "the leaves fall . . . winter has already come . . . but where is he, where is my love . . . he left without a kiss, not even a farewell . . ." His teeth started chattering, what shit was it he'd told her? He had to remember. Some other place, not in the cornfield, he'd promised her that when they gave her a party for receiving her teaching degree he would attend and he'd say, "Thank you very much for becoming a teacher," and he'd arrive with a present, a useful thing for their future home, for the two of them, is that clear? A useful thing with his name engraved on it. And he'd also promised her that when he completed his course in electricity, and after that in civil construction, he would be a good builder, so he could build their own home, with a garden, plants, all that stuff, preferably a white house with grainy walls, that kind of thing. But that's when they got into their biggest battle, she wanted smooth walls. And he explained how to make the plaster so that it will stay like that, one part with more granules than the other, and she, "No, not like that because it catches dust." And he, "No, I prefer it like that, I like it, it's a little harder to clean, but a man likes a hardworking woman." So she, "Hell, maybe it'll be all right!" Because she's a very sexy woman, is that clear? She likes sex a lot, because there are two kinds of women: the ones who were born to be housewives, to work and nothing else, not to be mounted, and the ones who were born to work and be mounted, which is to say, she's the kind of woman who was born to work and to be mounted. And he did his first job in town, very well built and everyone in the world liked it, yes? Because he worked while he was studying, he went there to study cement calculations, how much wire carries this and that, all that business, even how to calculate how many bricks in a house, and how many fucking pounds of this or that, and now he remembers one thing he said to her, something he'd forgotten, which he always told her. "The first nights we're married we're going to sleep far apart," could that be what she's asking about now? And she, "No, no, I want us to sleep together right from the first night," and he, "The first nights we're going to sleep very far apart, to see if you come looking for me, is that clear? The first nights we're married." But she didn't understand, and he, "The first night you're going to sleep in a separate room." It was to see if she'd get up the courage to look for him and that sort of things. At night he'd sleep in another room to see if she'd make some sign of love, then she'd come, she'd see him sleeping and start caressing him. So then he'd be waiting for her, not sleeping, one, two in the morning, she doesn't come and he's waiting, dawn breaks, patience, he'd go to work. And another day would go by, he'd leave for work, come back at night, go to sleep, far away from her, until she'd start feeling lonely and come looking for him, yes? And that's how the nights would pass, one after the other, always waiting for her to come looking for him, because he wouldn't go looking for her for anything in the world. Until the day she felt so lonely that she had to go to him in that way, right? Because they were living just as friends, he'd arrive, take a bath, have dinner, she'd go to her room, he to his, to see who could stand it alone longer, he or she, but he had sworn he'd never look for her, it had to be her. To see if she had courage, if she would get that aroused, is that clear? Because he would bring her a different present every day to build her excitement, then he'd move closer every time, to her, who kept getting those presents, any little present, a toy anything, today a small bottle of perfume, tomorrow a pacifier for the child, the future child they were going to have, all that kind of thing, and some other day a bar of soap, "Here is a little bar of soap for your child, for you to keep as a gift for your future child," and days passed, and another time he brought her a nightgown, something of that kind. He'd arrive, he'd put it on her himself, first he'd undress her and leave her in her panties, nothing else, and he'd put on the nightgown but without handling her, without the slightest possibility of riding her, he had to keep her at a certain distance, it was a war of love, a war to increase the love, one searching for the other one. And he'd also promised her that when they started he'd show her he was a strong young man, they could run five or six races a night. Back then he could make that type of calculation, yes? And there at the door of the bar you could hear the song coming from the park. He started walking over, slowly, and a guy with the initial such and such dedicated it to so-and-so in such and such a dress, and as that song was ending you'd hear another one. He ran into a teammate from before, but he said he was in a hurry, he had a lot to do. And that song ended and when he turned the corner and saw the park, everything the way it used to be, the slides and the swings for the little ones to play on and he heard the same thing again, the same record as before, "the leaves fall . . . winter has already come . . . but where is he, where is my love . . . he left without a kiss, not even a farewell . . . like those leaves blowing with the wind. . . ." And it was she, he was sure, it was she who'd asked them to repeat that record, he'd ask for another one to answer her, one that said different things, "You never heard of me again . . . but I kept seeing you anyhow . . . in all of this nostalgia that remained . . . so much time has already passed . . . but I never forgot you. . . . So many times I thought of coming back . . . and telling you my love has never changed . . . but silence was all that could be heard . . . and far away I die each day . . . without you ever knowing. . . ." He didn't go up to where they were playing records because there were people there who knew him and he didn't want to start saying hello to everyone, he just wanted to see if she was there. Someone requested a record, he watched from the corner and didn't see her; what was it he said to her that he can't remember now? One day she dedicated a record to him, "To the young man with long hair, chestnut colored, chestnut eyes, white complexion, Round the World shirt and black pants, black shoes, wristwatch, from a young lady with the initial M." And in Baurú he had heard something he liked on television and when he met her he would tell her all about it, he was going to ask her to be like the ideal wife they were talking about on television, because the situation is as follows: "For me the woman has to be the following, she should consider the man as if he were a friend, an excellent friend, is that clear? Never think he's her husband, yes? Live life as two friends, in the home, and the same with father and child, good friends, very intimate, everything out in the open so that the children learn everything the father tells them: Son, this is the way things are, explain the way the world works nowadays." In his day it wasn't like that, you leave the book open, with whoever, with the wife, with the children. The children and the wife, equal to the father, everyone equal, is that clear? Leave the book in sight completely open, he thinks it's much clearer that way, with nothing hidden, yes? Because hell, in this world if someone doesn't teach you, later in the street they don't teach you either. He heard the loudspeaker about two blocks away, the young man answering to the initial W requests that the following record be dedicated to a young lady in green with blue earrings, ". . . you never heard of me again . . . but I kept seeing you anyhow . . . in all of this nostalgia that remained . . . so much time has already passed . . . but I never forgot you. . . . So many times I thought of coming back . . . and telling you my love has never changed. . . ."

—I had something very important to tell you, too, but I forgot, I can't remember what it was anymore.

And he watched the mother one day when she had rheumatic pains, not the kind from giving birth, and he didn't know what to say to cheer her up, and the mother was looking at him, because he wanted to say something very meaningful, to solve her problems, but he didn't know what to say, "Oh, my son, I don't know what to do!"

And right then it didn't seem like her speaking, it seemed like someone who was dying, "You're putting so much affection into fixing up this little house in Santísimo, it's such a perfect name, always at home Saturday and Sunday fixing everything up." In Cocotá the father watches the sky for clouds, because he gets very nervous when it doesn't rain, he watches the grass dying of drought. The plants and the fields are dying. So the father gets sick, yes? He curses the whole world, "Hell, it's not going to rain this year!" And from that moment he starts to lose hope. If it rains when the son goes to work in Rio de Janeiro in those neighborhoods with tall buildings, the traffic gets all screwed up, but out on the farms the whole world is happy, because rain makes grapes, bananas, rice. Then the father whistles, he sings, he's completely different, his hope returns. The hope of finding her, and if he finds Gloria around there he's going to tell her to run away with him, in the morning on the first bus without anyone knowing, even though he doesn't remember what it was he said that she does remember, what was it? He doesn't remember but if he finds her he'll say something else she always liked, he used to say, "What pretty long hair! So blond it looks like shining gold, now I don't need a mirror because I look at myself in that mirror, it's so clean." And one day they did it when no one was looking, her hair went around his neck three or four times. They tied themselves together, that night, they wound themselves completely up in her hair, and in his, because back then he was a long-hair, a fashionable guy, and sometimes his hair got tangled up with hers, and it

seemed they'd never be able to get untied from one another again, ". . . so many times I thought of coming back
. . . and telling you my love has never changed . . . but
silence was all that could be heard . . . and far away I die
each day . . . without you ever knowing. . . ." And he
went into a new supermarket that he hadn't seen before,
it wasn't big but it was new, to buy tobacco, and it seemed
that someone was there in the back, so he went out to the
street without buying anything and after a while she came
out, María da Gloria; it looked to him like she had a
packet of sugar in her hand. So he said to her, "How are
you? I'm glad to see you!" And she was so emotional
she couldn't say anything, and she looked at the ground
and then went running home. He didn't say anything else
to her, was he wrong? Should he have stopped her and
talked to her more? He doesn't know why but he let her
go home. And he never saw her again. He went to the
park the next Thursday and she wasn't there either, and
the day he'd arrived from Mato Grosso he went back to
the farm and the mother asked him if he'd seen María da
Gloria, and he told her the truth, "I ran into her at the
entrance to the supermarket, I said hello to her, 'What's
going on? How are you?' that's all I said, she got so emotional she stopped dead in her tracks, she wanted me to
keep up the conversation, but I cut it off right there, I
didn't insist, I stopped right there, and so she didn't know
what to do and I left." And his father had seen him in the
field in the morning and they gave each other a big hug,
but now in the afternoon the old man was all dressed and
bathed, he didn't come over to converse with him and the

mother, he watched them from afar, but he smiled at the son. And later the son saw that the father was crying, but he didn't know what to do. What could he say? And the father went and cut some roses, the ones that they sell, and he went up to the son and gave them to him. And usually in the afternoon when the two of them were alone the father would keep looking at him and cry; he was very changed, he didn't hit the bottle anymore because the doctor had forbidden it. And the father didn't say anything, could it be because he remembered when he'd grabbed the shotgun, or worse, the cleaver, and wanted to kill someone there in the kitchen? The day the son returned to Mato Grosso the father went and cut even more roses, he treated him differently, he considered him as a son, and he didn't say anything, he kept looking at him, now the son was an honest working man.

—I know that very well. That's why I keep waiting for you.

Chapter Eleven

—How long has it been since you've been to Cocotá, son?

He hasn't been back to Cocotá in five years. Today he brought the mother one of those big steaks, the kind he likes, to forget about his troubles, and ground beef for her, the best, no fat. He collected a debt for a fucking window from hell they've owed him a heap of time. But it's not enough for the new treatment, he knows very well a hundred windows together wouldn't be enough.

—No one asked me anything, how your work was going, it's that the people from that town are the envious type. They must think you're playing ball and earning a lot and it makes them mad.

He gets home and when the mother starts talking he leaves, he goes out to the backyard, he goes to the bar. Today he's very tired, he doesn't even feel like taking a bath; he went all the way to Copacabana to collect that bill and he left the house at six in the morning and he just got back and it's ten at night, he can't move from this bed, he's worn out, dying of exhaustion, they were closing the butcher shop, the one in Copacabana and he just made it in to buy himself the steak, because they close at eight at night now. And he couldn't sleep on the bus.

—I didn't realize I'd run out of rice, but it'll be ready in a little while now, don't go to sleep otherwise who'll get you up later, and a man has to eat. While I'm on the subject, there's still so much I haven't told you about back there. You're always pretending to be asleep, or going to the bar, don't you like a little chat with the poor old lady anymore? I won't tell you anything sad, I know you don't like me complaining. Your poor father, he didn't ask about anything, not even how you were, but he was listening whenever I told your sisters anything. A son always loves the father, no matter how much he doesn't say so, yes? It's the law of the blood. It's better that you don't see him, sick as he is, he's gotten so old you wouldn't believe it. As ye sow so shall ye reap, they say. I never finished telling you about that girl, who used to be sick, but there are good people who should never have to die, the situation is grave with Olga's grandmother, I went to see her, she almost doesn't recognize anyone, Teresa always takes care of her, the son looks like the little black, Zilmar never saw him?

He doesn't answer, he pretends he's asleep. She'll shut her mouth, she won't keep talking by herself.

—We sure did a lot of talking, Teresa and me, she has another little kid, from someone in town, this one is a girl and she turned out very white, and the son of the little black is black as coal. And poor Teresa was crying because when the old lady dies she doesn't know what they'll do with the house, she'll have to live over there with Olga's parents. She's not going to marry this other one either, but he's a grown man already, the little black was fifteen years old when he gave her a child, and who was feeding him? How could he take care of this child! Patience, everything in order, I never cared for her much but just the same I asked about Azucena, but nobody knows anything about her, her father died and she went back to her mother's house and they went to another town, to live for good, but no one knows anything and she didn't leave from disgrace, expecting a child, or anything like that, she wasn't expecting anything. Teresa said that the two best people she'd ever known in her life were the old lady and Azucena, and one of them had left town and the old lady was about to go to the other world and she was alone in life to raise those two children. Everyone in the world has good recollections of Azucena, everyone says she was good, probably she was exactly like that and I was wrong, she seemed like some so-and-so to me, the way she chased after you all day. It's not because her mother was a servant, because she was a very decent woman, the mother. A woman shouldn't go around giving herself away like that, she'll always come to no good.

And I told Teresa to take care of herself, because that man from town comes to see her every once in a while and he could get her with child again, I told her to take the medicine, to take care of herself. And she's not the same Teresa now, she looks like an older woman already, and she's just twenty-nine years old. And I'd seen the one who used to be sick around town from afar, but one day I went to Olga's house and I saw her close up, and she waved to me. I was afraid she'd come over to talk and get an attack of nerves, but she waved and went into the house, she was coming from school with books and things. But they'd already told me at Olga's house that María da Gloria was better, she was pretty healthy because she went back to school, since last year, now. And what she doesn't do is go to dances, or she wasn't going.

Then he asked the mother something or other, if it had rained more this year than last, hadn't it? And if the father would be able to fix the roofs, once the pumpkins were harvested.

—He's very changed, your father isn't like he used to be, he doesn't watch all day now to see if it's going to rain, if clouds are gathering, and if there's water in the moon. He works all day, poor thing, slowly, but he's already out before it gets light, he doesn't have even one cow, I don't know why he gets up so early. I'd get up with him and I'd always be the first one at the hospital. And I'd wait for the doctor to arrive, even though sometimes the worst thing is to sit, for those of us who bear the cross of rheumatism, a very heavy cross, but there at the hospital you see a lot worse, and you accept what God sent you, those women come in so skinny, to take some treatment, they're yellow, they look like they haven't got long to live. And one morning I saw her, she was coming with another little girl from school, but much younger than her, because she lost all those years and now she's twenty-six she told me. At first I thought they were I don't know who, the other little girl, and the ones who showed up later. I thought they were the ones who went with her to take the cure for her nerves. Ones her mother had gotten to go with her. But later she told me they were companions from school and that they'd come to be vaccinated, on orders from the people at the school. I saw her coming and said hello because she'd greeted me very sincerely when I saw her from the sidewalk of Olga's house. And then she seemed happy that I'd said hello to her and she came over to talk to me, I'd stayed seated where people wait for the doctor. And she gave me a kiss, and how many years since she'd seen me? Then I told her that I'd come here to Santísimo years ago and that your father wanted to leave the farm because it never rained and he'd had no luck, but he didn't like being a stevedore in the port, he liked that even less, and he wanted to come back but I stayed to take care of the son, who was still single, or that's what you kept saying around but you certainly had married by the church and by everything, even though you were separated, and then she looked at me straight in the eyes, but then she lowered her eyes. I thought she was getting ready to say something and then she didn't. Who knows what? And I told her you'd left the job at ECSP and you'd come here to Santísimo to see if you could get ahead working not as a mason, but doing harder things, that a mason alone couldn't do, because you hadn't forgotten what you learned in school in Cocotá, and you could do the work of a well-qualified mason, more than that, what the handymen do, and with some assistant you'd gotten you did very good work, but it was a life of sacrifice because it's two hours from Santísimo, almost, to the neighborhoods where there's always work, in the better parts of Rio. And then she asked what happened to me to be in the hospital, since I seemed very healthy, always a little fat, which is a good sign of health and all that. And then I told her it was to see if they could give me another rheumatism treatment, less expensive, and that they'd recommended that I not work too much and rest, so the question was whether I'd go back to Cocotá for good, where my oldest daughter could take care of me, even though she has that whole heap of kids, but I didn't tell her anything about having to sell this house if there was no other choice. That I don't tell anyone, because my heart sinks just to think about it. And she told me that if I went back to Cocotá to live I should stop by and see her one day, even though I wouldn't be working at Olga's house anymore, one day I could go up to her house. And I told her no, because the mother wouldn't like it because I'd never worked outside my house until there was no choice and I was a servant in Olga's house all those years. And that I knew my place and I didn't like to go to a house where people weren't used to it, to someone who'd been a servant before in the house across the street. And she told me she knew my family hadn't been servants, but life is like that, when you have to work there's no choice, and that she knows very well that life is sure to teach you not to be so proud, and things like that. Then I got up the nerve to ask her what she was doing there at the hospital. And she told me it was for the vaccination and all that. And that this year she gets her teaching degree, that she's a little embarrassed being with the other younger ones, like ten years younger, because she couldn't study all those years, but now she's fine. And I asked her why she didn't go out more, a pretty girl like her, because I remembered that Olga's mother had told me she didn't go to the dances, not even to the park on Thursday's. And María da Gloria smiled a little and didn't answer at all, like that, she told me something or other, to leave me thinking. And then I felt like telling her that it wasn't right, what happened, that everyone in town was mad at you because they blamed you for causing everything, that she'd gotten sick from nerves, although there were a lot of people who blamed her parents, who didn't want to see you going out with her secretly. And I felt like telling her that that's why I hadn't let you two go into the shed on the farm that night, because I knew her parents didn't like you, that you were still very young and you hadn't made your own way in life yet.

He asked the mother if she'd hidden the cigarettes, yes? He couldn't find them, although he couldn't remember if he'd forgotten and left them at the construction site or not, had he? But he's over his cold now and if she'd hidden them she had to give them back now, one or two cigarettes wouldn't make him sick, is that clear?

—I didn't hide anything from you, you're always saying that; I hid them from you when you had a fever, that other time, but this time I didn't hide anything. Your father keeps smoking, too, I'm tired of telling him it's bad for him, already. You know what? Somebody told me to send you his regards. Your father was the one who told me Matías was back in town, and he did ask your father, "And Josemar? What's Josemar doing?" Because Matías is an agronomist, just like María da Gloria's brother, and they were at the farm because the landowner asked them to look at some cane fields that are always drying out and all that. I didn't get up the nerve to ask María da Gloria anything there at the hospital because Olga and the mother told me that some people already know about it but that they still don't want many people to know, and it's that Matías was on his vacation, he lives in Minas Gerais where he's working on some very big corn fields around there. Matías can't go to Cocotá except on vacation because he can't leave work. And that kind of thing.

He asked the mother who sent him regards.

—Matías sends you many regards; he said to your father, And how's Josemar? How's Josemar doing? Because he has a good recollection of what a good boy you were, and this and that, and that nobody played better ball. And those kinds of things you say from your heart.

He asked the mother something, he was very tired,

sprawled on the bed, he looked at the wall because his eyes hurt from arranging little mosaics just so all day long, all he could look at was the wall, the mother had the light on next to the stove to heat up the iron before throwing on the steak. He had his back to her but he asked her something, if Matías had married, or if he was going to get married.

—Matías doesn't have another girlfriend, no. It seems there's no one else. Olga's mother says he's better than most men, he has a mustache, and he's not as fat as he used to be. And María da Gloria's mother doesn't tell that to anyone, but she places a lot of trust in Olga's mother, and she told her that when Matías arrived it had been years since he'd seen María da Gloria, because he'd been living with them because he was the son of a friend that had been left a widower and Matías was there in Cocotá, but when he left to study agronomy he didn't come back on vacations and now when he found María da Gloria much better, now that she was going to school, he began to talk with her a lot, and keep her company a lot, because she didn't want to go out anywhere by herself, to walk around, yes? And one day she went for a walk with him, the family trusted him completely, as if he were a brother, and the parents were happy to see that she wanted them to bring her some new little bird for her cages, she used to have so many and later when she got sick she didn't want them anymore. And some say she let them out of the cage, Olga told me no, she gave some of them to her, because they brought back bad memories, or they made her sad, not bad memories, I didn't mean that. But there were people who said other things. Teresa told me and swore to me that she saw María da Gloria grab the little birds from the cage and squeeze them in her hand until their bones cracked, that she even pulled their bones apart. I don't believe her, she hated her because Teresa was a close friend of Azucena's, wasn't she? You can't believe her because she's in the enemy camp. And Matías also took her to the park on Thursday, and her face had more color, she wasn't so pale, Olga's mother says that for years and years she was deathly pale, because of the nighttime business, not being able to rest well at night. And one place she never again set foot in was the dance, but now she made herself a new dress and went.

—He asked the mother one thing, he asked her not to make the steak especially for him; if she made something for herself, OK, if not, why bother? Because he wasn't hungry and in a little while he was going to the bar. And he wanted to know one thing, what color was the new dress that girl made.

—She didn't tell me or I don't remember. But they insisted in the household, or Matías talked her into it. And she went. And now the problem is that they had a job ready for María da Gloria in the school, as soon as she'd received her teaching degree, to teach the very smallest little ones, because she seems to be very patient and she requested it. So that job was reserved for her, and other girls from around there complained, they'd already gotten their degrees a year, two years before, and they were still waiting for work. And Teresa told me this, and it's a

girl from the countryside around there, from very poor
people, that had already gotten her degree, I don't know
if it was one year or two before, and they finally offered
her a teaching job but very far away, like three hours,
and right in the middle of the country, way out, which
didn't matter to her because she was born and raised in
the country, but she had to live more than one hundred
miles away alone in that school with one other girl. All
right, but what happened is, she found out that there was
this teaching position in Cocotá itself, and they'd reserved
it when the old teacher retired that year, they'd reserved
it for Gloria who'd had so many trials and who was supposed to have graduated years before. And what happened is this one from the country, I don't know if you'd
remember her, she was a little kid when you were there,
Pascual Gonçalves's daughter, and this one found out
that Gloria was probably not going to take the teaching
position in Cocotá, and before she signed the ministry
papers to go to that little school in the country she wanted
to know if Gloria was going to accept the position or not.
Because this is what I'm telling you, that it was her turn,
if it wasn't for Gloria, who has the advantage that her
family was from there in town and all that, and what I
already told you about. And the thing is that finally this
one that I'm telling you about, her name is Regina,
Regina Gonçalves, got the position in town, because
Gloria isn't going to take it, because then Olga's mother
and Olga say it's because Matías asked them for her hand
and they didn't want to say anything to anyone so there
wouldn't be gossip again like the other time. I don't

know, I don't like people like that, myself, hypocrites, but then with all that happened I've changed my mind a little and I feel the same as Olga, that Gloria really did love you and that it wasn't her fault, it was her family's. Olga always defends you, she doesn't come to visit the mother every day, the mother complains a lot, that she's nearby and that Olga's husband has a car and that she doesn't come by every afternoon at least to give her a kiss. But Olga was always like that, she's lazy and with the twins she doesn't feel like budging to go anywhere. They say her house is all modernized, I never went there, I don't know if you'd remember how your father got if we went by that house. Such a beautiful house. And Olga's right not wanting to budge from there, to stay in her precious house always, with her children and her husband, but it's selfish not going to see the mother. Olga's mother says she gets gloomy in the afternoons from being alone, and with the grief of having her mother-in-law so sick, she's going to die one of these days. And I told her she should bring Teresa to the house, but Olga's mother said she didn't like that guy, Teresa keeps seeing him, after he gets her with child and doesn't give her a cent to raise him with, and she keeps seeing him. Of course Teresa doesn't tell anyone but they see the guy hanging around the old lady's house at night. And Teresa herself told me so, that she sees him, because she really does love him. I'm sure Azucena must have ended up the same way, but no one knows where she is, and when they left town she didn't have a belly or anything. But Olga's mother was always like that, pretty selfish, and she doesn't care about Teresa, and Olga's just like her mother. Now the mother-in-law was truly a saintly woman, I think she must have died already, because the week before I came the priest had already been to see her and all, poor thing, what a good woman, how she won people's hearts. And Olga turned out more like the mother than like the father's family, but she's a good girl, I always loved her, probably because I watched her grow up, and someone who's worked in the house all those years knows everything, even the biggest secrets. And she made me swear on a stack of Bibles not to tell you this, but I think I'd better tell you, so you can see that there are people there still who have a lot of affection for you. One day Olga came to her mother's house and I'd gone over there to do the cooking because Olga's mother asked me to because she was going to be with the mother-in-law, the day the priest went, and Olga, at the last minute, didn't want to go with her, she stayed with me because she didn't want to go with her children, they're so noisy, to a house where a person is dying. I think it's because it hurt her so much to see the grandmother dying, such a loving woman. So the two of us were left alone, the little ones were out playing in the backyard. And Olga asked me never to tell you, but she was going to tell me so I could see what a good son I had. And then she began. I already knew, and who didn't, that since she was little she adored you, but that's kid stuff, but she was very naughty, and advanced for her age, and she developed sooner than any other girl. And then she told me that she'd always loved you, but like a real woman, she had the guts to tell me that, she

saw what a pretty boy you were, and still are, I told her,
that you're always the same, well-groomed, with a well-
trimmed beard, but when a kid develops all at once she's
a woman, she loses her head and if she falls in love with
some man she's capable of doing all kinds of craziness if
the mother isn't there watching over her. That's why I
never let your sisters go anywhere alone at that age, later
at fifteen or sixteen years old the heart's something else
again. And Olga said she spent hours spying on you when
you were with Gloria, because Gloria's father got in late
and Gloria's mother let you do anything you wanted if
you went into the garden and no one on the street could
see, she didn't want that. But just the same they knew in
town that you were making out, because at the dance you
danced together a lot, even though the mother brought
her there and back. And Olga spied on you and she was
dying of jealousy, and she says that one day when the
brothers were playing with you they began throwing
pillows on top of you, because you were much stronger
and bigger, in age too, and in a moment of confusion like
that she kissed you on the mouth. And with all the trust
they'd given you in her household you could have taken
advantage, because it was a big house with a lot of places
to hide and she was always provoking you to go behind
the fruit trees. Like after school you would come for me
to give you lunch with them, they were going to a different school but at the same time, and later it was worse,
when it was dark out, when you came back to walk me
home after I'd washed the dinner dishes. But you never
paid attention to her because you had respect for the

household, and I think also because you only had eyes
for the one across the street, and then there was that other
tramp, Azucena, the shameless one. They can go and defend her, but Teresa always told me about everything both
of you did. But then Olga sure did leave me with my mouth
hanging open with what she told me, I don't know how
she had the nerve to tell me, Olga is a girl with a lot of
character. And it happened like this, she says that one
night, the last one, because the next day you left without
saying good-bye to anyone, that night she was spying as
usual while you were making out with Gloria and she
heard her crying, and so instead of spying from her house
she went out and crossed the street because she wanted to
hear what you were saying behind the hedge. And when
she got there, Olga, you were already separating from
Gloria, in a fight, and when you left, Gloria always used
to go up to her balcony and watch until you turned the
corner, or until you went into Olga's house if I had dinner
ready. But that night Gloria went into the house because
she had broken with you forever, and so there was Olga
hidden behind some bushes and she called you. And instead of going in the front door of her house she made
you go in between some bushes where the wire fence was
broken and she said she wanted to talk to you. And you
were so sad and so upset, Olga told me, that your hands
were shaking, and you practically couldn't speak. And
now I'm ashamed to continue, even though a mother
shouldn't be ashamed, with a son, who is flesh of her flesh,
but so, this you'll know better than anyone, she began to
want to console you, and there in the back of the garden

she took off her underwear and gave it to you to smell, she put her mother's perfume on it, hoping one day you'd notice what a pretty perfume she wore, and there you were and she herself took down your pants, like I did when you were little and you had to sit down to do your little poop, and she started trembling with fear because it was the first time she'd have a man on top of her, and then you told her it was wrong, what you were doing, and you didn't want to continue. And you saved her honor forever. And if you hadn't been like that she wouldn't even have a fraction of what she has now. She says she never would have noticed her husband because she liked the bigger ones, mature men already, but she knew he was the son of a man even richer than her father and that the boy's father owned the farms and we were always telling her he was a very good man, too bad your father didn't like him because of that gossip. And when this little boy grew up she began to like him a lot and she says, Olga, that he looks a lot like you, that's why she first started to look at him, and I told her all pretty boys look a little alike, and Olga said yes, that's why. And now she's a lady, to me she's always the kid she used to be, the most mischievous in the world, worse than any of my children, but I look at her and see that she's every bit a lady now, living in that big luxurious house, which I never set foot in again, it's more than thirty years since we used to bring the season's first basket of peaches to the deceased mother of the owner as a present, she liked apricot peaches so much. The landowner was still single and your father had that jealous fit. Olga has everything in life, and with those two children so pretty you wouldn't believe it. And she hugged me and told me she owed it all to you, because if you'd taken advantage of her that night, she had become so brazen, her life would have ended that night, like what happens to good women who make a big mistake in this world. And instead that night was when life began for her, Olga told me, until that night she'd been a mischievous kid, and already almost without shame, but thanks to the respect you had for her that night she became a woman.

He'll say he has to go out and find cigarettes, and then he'll go to the bar because he's not hungry, he doesn't want anything to eat. And luck goes with those who deserve it, this afternoon the people from that apartment out in Copacabana paid him for that fucking window, and he had enough for a beer and enough to stand the unemployed guys there to a beer, they're playing dice with dry throats for sure. Guys poorer than hell, without one cruzeiro to buy themselves a good drink.

Chapter Twelve

He didn't have to sign any papers because everything was in his mother's name, he didn't even miss a day of work or any shit, he admits it and doesn't complain, because the mother went to the notary's office by herself and later she told him that the mother of his children went with her. She turned up for a visit and the mother asked her to go with her to sign for the sale of the house, her glasses aren't good anymore and she knows how to read but now she can't see with those glasses, and she doesn't know how to write but she can sign her name. And she'll take care of the check, no one will steal it, she'll take it to Cocotá and put it in the bank there and that way she'll keep taking out whatever she needs for the treatment. His sisters will take care of her there, all that kind of thing, and what's the fuss, there wasn't any other fucking way, he has to go to work every morning and she'd be alone if she had an attack of something. And one month is more than enough time for him to find some kind of room around there. Because everything's gone to hell, but it wasn't his fault, he never stopped working, not even for one day that he can remember.

—Son, have you fallen asleep already? . . . I don't feel well, my back is hurting, I can't stand it anymore. Will it be bad for me if I take the medicine again?

The mother didn't want to sell the house, and he, "If you want to worry, go ahead and worry, that's your problem, I don't have any problem; you're sick so sell it and take care of your health with the money and life will just go on." And on his same street they're going to auction off a piece of land, they told him that in Santísimo it's going for two hundred and fifty, three hundred thousand cruzeiros, cash, is that clear? And it's a good deal, to buy, that way you don't keep paying rent, for what, for the rest of your life? It's fucked, this business. That's why people go crazy, yes? This confusion starts up in his head because he doesn't have the cash for even one fucking installment, and if you buy the land you still have to build the house, no? If he had a friend he'd tell him to buy, because it's a good price, if he had a very good friend who would lend him something he wouldn't miss the chance, isn't that true? What little he had was that house and he's going to lose that, what? He's lost it already! Because while he had that little bit of money in seventy-six he didn't let it slip through his fingers, he had a firm grip on that cash, but then his mother's operation came up and since it was so dangerous it was better to pay than go to the free hospital, but the mother realized that these few last days he gets home and he's very changed, he hardly has anything to say, he's not in a joking mood. It was just one little room with the kitchen right there. And, with the father, they built another room, and the bathroom. And just last Sunday he put in a pipe to bring water right in from the street. The father paid fifteen hundred cruzeiros, which is now fifteen hundred cents, Goddamnit.

—I hardly did a thing all day, heavenly virgin, I kept still all day, why do I have to have an attack of pain like this? I'd rather die than suffer like this.

This person has a car, but he's forced to sell it, and that same person likes the car, he sells it only as a last resort, when he doesn't even have enough cash to eat or even for a glass of water, and that's the case with her, his mother, because the consultations with the doctor are very expensive, the analyses they do, examination of this and examination of that, all of it's very expensive and the doctors themselves charge a lot, and the free hospital isn't any good, they end up killing you. And he asked her to leave him a picture, but if she forgets she might as well just take it, he's not going to go around begging for anything. María da Gloria never saw the picture of his mother when she was a kid, eight years old, a colored postcard, it wasn't a picture of herself, because the family was poor and they didn't take pictures out in the country, it was a postcard somebody had bought, but his mother, one day she saw it and she asked someone if she could have it because she thought she looked the same when she was a kid. He already asked her for it, and if the mother asks him again what he wants her to leave him as a keepsake he's not going to tell her again, if she remembers, fine, if not who cares, what the fuck!

—The medicine doesn't help at all, why are you so quiet tonight?

María da Gloria was always asking him questions when they were going together, "What do you hate most about the farm where you always lived?" And he said, the prickly plant, if a guy goes by thinking about something else he can really hurt himself, and then she asked him, "And what do you like and feel most affection for on the farm?" And if María da Gloria asked him what he hates most about this house in Santísimo he was thinking about it and he doesn't know what it could be. And once she also asked him what he hated most about Olga's grandmother's house, because she didn't say anything but she knew he was going there, that he went in almost every night with Azucena. And he said what he hated most was a nail in a window, and she didn't know why and he didn't tell her either, because one time when he was going in through the window he caught his pants and ripped them. And what he liked most about the landowner's house was the soccer field, because when he'd go near there and the owner would see him when he was little, he'd slipped away from his father, the landowner would say, "Let's play a little ball, I'll show you how to make moves," and this and that. And he showed him and when he got big he was the best player and everyone asked him, "Where did you learn to play like that?" And what he liked best about Olga's house was the kitchen where they'd made so many good beefsteaks, the kind he likes. And what he hated most about Gloria's house was that tree they always leaned against to make out, and where they were together that night for the last time.

—Thank God the medicine is beginning to relieve the pain, don't stay up, I think I'll go to sleep soon.

He can't sleep, he rolls onto one side, onto the other, he tries one position, he tries another position, today he played ball badly, he was thinking about something else, he couldn't even make a good move, could he?

—Tomorrow is Monday and you have to get up early again, it's time for you to go to sleep.

He hasn't got even one bill left for the bus to work tomorrow, he'll take it from the mother while she isn't looking, misery of shit! He hasn't even not worked one single day in his life, fucking shitty luck! And tonight he won't be able to sleep, he too has something inside closing tighter every time, like a fist.

—What's wrong, son, why are you tossing and turning like that? Why aren't you resting? If you don't gather your strength at night you won't be able to work the next day.

He didn't answer her, he's not even going to answer the mother because if he starts talking he'll say whatever shit comes into his head.

—I know what's wrong with you, it's that you're never going to forgive me for selling the house and leaving you without anything, even if it's not my fault. . . . And I'm going to die of that shame, it's worse than any sickness. . . .

Shitty old woman! Whore! Filthy rotten old woman! It's all your fault, you vile old hag, she was going into the shed, she loved me, she'd made up her mind that day, and I was going to get her pregnant, good and pregnant! That was my plan! After that the parents couldn't say a thing. But you scared her that day, she repented, don't you realize that? And you made her feel like a whore, she was finally going to give it to me that day, she'd saved it for me, and after that I could never talk her into it again, and she started telling me the mother told her I was the little boyfriend to play with, when she was a kid, that's all, but now she was a young lady and she had to think of her future and if the father found out we were there together every night he'd get mad for real. And I started telling her that if she didn't love me because I was poor then we might as well leave each other once and for all. And she, no, no, she loved me. And one night I arrived, are you listening to me, you old whore? And her head was bowed, looking at the ground, and she told me the mother had forbidden her to see me ever again, because if not she would tell the father, and then it was really all over, wasn't it? And it didn't matter so much that I was poor, the son of the servant from the house across the street, but the bad thing is that I didn't do anything, I didn't help my father, and I said, if you call that a father. And that I went to the masonry school in the morning and all afternoon I wandered around doing nothing, saying I was the best ball player, and its true I was the best, is there anything wrong with that? And at night mixed up with women, yes? Because the whole world knew about Azucena, and because of you more than anything, you went around telling the whole world, couldn't you keep quiet? No! You filthy old hag! Why don't you just die and once and for all, all this crap about suffering is worse than death! But you don't die! And that's why they said I was a scoundrel, an opportunist, that Azucena is stained now forever. And so it seems Gloria's mother regretted having trusted in me, and that's what she said, according to Gloria, that I'd taken advantage of the fact that I was the son of the servant and in Olga's house they'd trusted me because of that, and because of that they let me inside the house and she saw that they let me into Olga's house, so then she let me in, too, but now enough is enough, is that clear? If she sees her with me again she'll tell the father everything. And that was your work, disgusting old woman! And he told Gloria he was going to mount her right there and she told him he had to change and become good, and work with his father in the country and when she was older she'd marry him, they both had to be patient and wait, but that the separation was a test of love and then he gave her a hell of a slap, which is how you have to treat all of you, whores and traitors all of you. And then she, what could she do? She started to cry and then she said she never wanted to see him again, and all in sobs she said she did love him and he didn't. And he left and he could have gotten Olga pregnant who was there waiting for him, but he didn't touch her, he doesn't know why. Anyway, it got

all screwed up, shitty old hag, whore daughter of the
biggest whore of the Indians!

—Son . . . if you're awake . . . please . . . that tablet,
the one I prepared, my sides are splitting from pain, I
can't get up.

Her sides are splitting from pain, she can't get up.
That's why she takes the medicine, and she asks for him
to hand it to her, and the daughters aren't there, he has
to hand it to her . . . or not? And now his mother also
knows he's not a scoundrel, an opportunist, yes? Olga
told her, but she's sick and I am the one who has to help
her get better, she has enough trouble already, he's a
man, is that clear? And he'll show everyone he's not a
scoundrel or an opportunist, is he?

—Thank you. . . . Were you having a bad dream? I
heard you tossing and turning in bed, restless as anything.

The landowner said to him one day, "Still a kid and
see how good your legs are getting already for playing
ball." And if he had enough for the fare now he'd go to
Cocotá and ask the landowner for some cash to buy the
land, and he'd say, "Won't you lend me some cash so I
can buy myself some land? I don't know how I'll pay you
back, but if I have any luck I'll play the lottery every
month." For sure the landowner would lend him the cash,
but he doesn't even have enough for the bus to work
tomorrow morning. So he'll have to take it out of the
mother's wallet, he had more than one beer after the game
this afternoon, yes?

—Why aren't you asleep yet? Did the kids make you
very nervous?

The mother of the two children was here again today, a special Sunday visit here, as he was leaving for the game. It was three in the afternoon, that's when she arrived. He didn't come back until eleven o'clock at night. When he got back she wasn't there anymore. She stayed and talked with his mother. He said to her, "With your permission I'm going to play ball, I have a very important game." So she turned to look at him and said, "To this day you haven't stopped with the ball; it's dangerous, if they hurt you you'll have to go to work on Monday tomorrow and you won't be able to." Which is what she always said, and he, "It's dangerous, but I like playing ball." And he left for the game and didn't come back until eleven at night. So after the game he and some others went to talk, to discuss the game and how the team was doing. Today they had a brilliant victory, seven to three, he made two goals, as usual, there isn't a game that he doesn't get his big goal in. And she said something to him, to fuck with him, because she's like that, always waging war with him, "Just like that you're going to play a game, and so on. . . . Don't you see you have a guest? Your children are here." So he hugged the kids and they started kissing him and asking him for sweets when he got back, when he came back from the game, same old business, is it clear what it's like? And she starts up again with the same thing, she earns nine thousand cruzeiros and the rent is five thousand, yes? After paying six hundred for light and water and drainage, you're cleaned out. And they have to eat with the four thousand he gives for support for the kids. Which he has to give, because

it's no joke, no sir. A father has to be a father, if not he
has no feelings. But that's the way it is, reality is like
that. If he had the cash there'd be no problem, he'd buy
a little land and build them a small house, he knows how
to build a house. But it's hard to get that cash together.

—If you can't sleep you can turn on the light, it won't
bother me.

He told the mother not to worry, he's fine, he's just not
tired, and that's all, yes? And he got up and put on his
pants. Then he went out to the backyard, and what he
hates most about that house is the gate, it gets stuck and
when he gets back tired he has to stand there and force
it. And what he likes best about that house is the trees,
the mango tree, the mangoes used to be very small, and
the banana trees. And there's the moon shining. When he
was twelve years old, thirteen years old he'd look at the
sky in the country and his head was full of plans. He
thought a lot of foolish things that people shouldn't think,
but also he did a lot that people shouldn't do. And when
people look at the sky they remember a lot of different
things, girlfriends, being a lot younger and all the things
that were happening, they remember their whole lives.
And the plans. One of the plans was to have his own car,
which he never had, shitty luck, and other important
business for him was to grow and be very tall. And be
well-dressed; and be a progressive guy, a guy who strug-
gles and contributes to progress, and who makes a lot of
cash. He didn't accomplish any of that, did he? Tall, yes,
he grew well like he wanted to. So when people look at
the moon they think of all that. He likes to look at the

sky and the stars because they're beautiful, but it's better in the countryside. Out in the country all you can see is the beautiful night, open country, where there aren't any lights, which ruin everything. There if a person looks up he'll see what a really beautiful sky looks like. And his mother seems to have fallen asleep, she's not complaining anymore, out in the backyard he can't hear her, yes? Tomorrow he'll take some cash from her, enough for the bus fare and that's all, and he's not sure that suffering is worse than death. Death is the worst there is. Death is a terrible thing. He wouldn't like to die, when a person dies that's the end of everything, females stay behind, friends stay behind, companions from work, the whole bunch. And people practically forget about the one who dies. A person has a good friend, he dies, and he remembers him for a while and then he starts to forget, like with Rogerio who died from a snake bite, he remembered Rogerio for a while and now it's been years since he's thought about Rogerio. A friend dies and a person makes other friends and forgets, that's death. Death is the worst there is, because if a person dies people forget about him.

—Josemar! Son . . . Don't catch cold, why did you go out without a coat like that? Come on, let's go inside, it's very chilly. I slept for awhile and the pain went away. . . . But then I woke up again, it must be that I felt like I had to tell you something. It's that tonight my back was hurting so much, so much that I remembered the pain of when you were born. And I remembered what I thought when I saw you for the first time. And it's that then when you were a newborn I thought one thing, just like that, for no reason, and it was that I was going to love you a lot, I don't know why, but more than my other children. And after a time I thought that was bad because you should love all your children the same. But later you grew up a little and I realized that you loved me more than the others in the family. Everyone loved me a lot when I gave them something, but if I didn't give them anything they didn't love me so much. But not Josemar, I thought, he loves me a lot just because he does, even if I don't give him a thing. And then years went by and it stayed like that. And tonight I was thinking, those poor other ones, if I don't give them anything they don't love me a lot, and it's because those poor ones, they're always in need of one thing or another, they don't have anything, but with Josemar people love him everywhere because he's so handsome, and he isn't always in need as much as the others because he's full of things, and of the affection of so many women who follow him around, some of them shameless, others not. And that's why he can love me so much and not ask for anything, because he doesn't have much money but he has other things, and it's as if he were rich.

Epilogue

He couldn't get up this morning because he slept so little last night, but standing on this shitty bus he can't even get a little sleep on the way to Rio. Luckily this week the fucking bathroom with its fucking tiles is finished. And then all that's left to do is put up the mirror. At least he'll be able to look at himself a little, so he can shave, because he didn't even have time for that with so much work and so much shit he doesn't even remember his own face. If he was sitting on the side with the window he could look at himself in the glass. Sometimes he forgets his own face.

—When was the last time you saw me?

He saw her for the last time ten, eight years ago. After that, only from afar. It was in Cocotá, the State of Rio.

In the uark next to the church, right? She went to meet him, they had a date, or—how was it? From there they left together, to the Municipal Club to dance all night. And what else happened with her? They were at the dance until two-thirty in the morning, then they went to a hotel to do their business, is that clear? That night.

—And no one noticed that a girl of fifteen was going to a hotel?

There were a lot of people in the club, the town wasn't very big, six thousand people, six thousand inhabitants. But it was possible to go to a hotel, no problem—not there, but in another town nearby, is that clear? They arrived, had a little beer, and so on. They went by car, back then he had a Maverick. Later, after he hit the skids, he never had a car again. Next year, God willing, he's going to buy one on credit.

—What dance was that?

It was a dance with Roberto Carlos music, nothing else, all night long Roberto Carlos records. There were also other places to make out. There was the swimming pool, for some terrific dips, and the waterfall. They climbed up the rocks, they put on bikini and bathing shorts and went into the trees—right there is the real jungle.

—I asked you about the dance, about the dance that night.

The dance was jam-packed, three or four thousand people. The two of them knew a lot of people, so many, but it was getting late, time to get moving. At the dance they were feeling terrific, satisfied, happy with life.

—And what did we talk about at the dance? I want to see if you're telling me the truth.

They talked about love, nothing but sweet talk. A little kissing, he made some moves, and then some more, to get them to leave the dance, because until then they'd never had a chance to go to a hotel, because she was still very young, a virgin, is that clear? And that Saturday it all started, she had a few drinks and they went to the hotel and well, that was the last time he saw her, isn't that right? That night of the dance and the next day. It was on the way back, returning from Floresta de Cocotá to Cocotá itself, which is another town, it was then that he made a date with her for eight-thirty the following evening, which was Sunday, at her house. But he didn't arrive until a quarter past eleven that night, and they stayed up talking, and fighting, and arguing. He wanted to escape from her, and the whole world was coming down on him—the mother, the grandmother were on his back, "Don't abandon my daughter!" That whole story, and he always slipping away, "No! I want to travel, I have to make my own way in life! After that, I'll come back for sure . . ." But he never came back. In all this time he never came around these parts, except once, in passing, isn't that so?

—That time you returned, could you see me from so far away?

That time he returned it seemed to him that he saw her; that she tried to get closer, but he moved away, right? But next time he's passing through he'll try to say something nice to her, drop a friendly word, just casually, is that clear? Just to ease that mental problem of hers, she hadn't been well in the head, everyone said. He remembers everything about that last night at the dance, down to the last detail. She showed up in a new green dress, a black ribbon in her hair, but he wasn't to be out done. He showed up in a pair of Lee jeans that had just come out then and a Round the World shirt. It was a very good-looking shirt, very few people had them, because they were expensive, is that clear?

—You hadn't thought of me for a long time, now luckily you've started to remember again.

At a certain hour they left the dance. Because that night she felt he was really serious about leaving town, that was when she gave it to him, thinking that way she'd tie him to her, "You're not leaving at all, you're staying here with me, aren't you?" Then he told her no, he was still leaving, is it clear how it went? But the truth is he didn't tell her he was going to abandon her that night, he knew her weak spots very well, he'd die before he'd tell her a thing like that. The important thing was to get her out of the dance, outside he'd take care of the rest. Then he put her in the car, already talking about the subject, "My love, we're going to another town, to enjoy some-thing new, what the hell. At last count we've been going together for three years, that's why I think I deserve a little trust, etcetera." Then she cried, she broke into loud sobs, but he didn't give an inch, he was going full steam, he'd had a few too many, right? They stayed on that road, they got to the room, took a shower, right? Her clothes were in a style that it was hard for her to get them

off. He got pretty mad. He grabbed her hard, "No!" she
screamed, "Get in bed, I tell you!" He put her in bed
and took off her clothes and they began kissing, biting
and stuff like that. She cried like crazy, desperately.
That's when he said to her, "Baby, it's useless, you
can't escape, the night is yours and you have to take
advantage of it." But she liked it too much that first time,
"You didn't like it that much because it hurt you a lot,
is that clear?" "No, the situation is as follows: I should
have listened to you, Josemar, and let you do it to me
the first day I met you." And then he said, "That's impossible because when I met you you were twelve years
old, or younger? Back then you must have been ten years
old. I never would have done that to you, is that clear,
now, yes, you're at a good age, even though it hurt you
just the same." He was crazy about her!

It's hard to remember everything, she was fifteen going
on sixteen, if he talks much about that subject he gets
that feeling that he wants to go see her, is that clear?
They spent many nights together making out, what the
fuck. First they walked around the square, then by all the
houses in the town, they'd walk around, really, it's true
that they walked around. Later they'd stay in her garden,
nice and dark, squeezing tight, until it got late. When he
left he'd turn around in the street and look at her window,
she'd be there as always, waving good-bye, until he'd
turn the corner with those very tall trees, ever taller than
he—far taller than he.